"The lon_____ away the kidnapper gets. I love my son even if you don't."

He dragged her against him, crushing her chest into his. "I love Jake more than life itself. He's my reason for living."

His move left her breathless, the feel of his body against hers more shocking than his accusations. "Okay, so you love him. What next?"

"We find him."

"Then what are you doing now?"

"Making a mistake," he said, staring down at her, his smoldering black eyes burning into hers. "But for some damned reason, I can't help myself."

"Then don't." She leaned up, pressing her lips to his, which started an avalanche of repercussions neither expected.

ELLE JAMES

BUNDLE OF TROUBLE

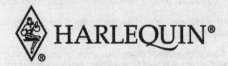

TORONTO • NEW YORK • LONDON
AMSTERDAM • PARIS • SYDNEY • HAMBURG
STOCKHOLM • ATHENS • TOKYO • MILAN • MADRID
PRAGUE • WARSAW • BUDAPEST • AUCKLAND

This book is dedicated to my wonderful editor,
Denise Zaza, for having faith in my writing
and helping me to grow as a Harlequin author.

Recycling programs
for this product may
not exist in your area.

ISBN-13: 978-0-373-69493-8

BUNDLE OF TROUBLE

Copyright © 2010 by Mary Jernigan

www.eHarlequin.com

Printed in U.S.A.

ABOUT THE AUTHOR

Golden Heart winner for Best Paranormal Romance in 2004, Elle James started writing when her sister issued a Y2K challenge to write a romance novel. She managed a full-time job, raised three wonderful children and she and her husband even tried their hands at ranching exotic birds (ostriches, emus and rheas) in the Texas Hill Country. Ask her and she'll tell you what it's like to go toe-to-toe with an angry 350-pound bird! After leaving her successful career in information technology management, Elle is now pursuing her writing full-time. She loves building exciting stories about heroes, heroines, romance and passion. Elle loves to hear from fans. You can contact her at ellejames@earthlink.net or visit her Web site at www.ellejames.com.

Books by Elle James

CAST OF CHARACTERS

Tate Vincent—Texas multimillionaire rancher who adopted a baby boy to satisfy his dying father's wish for grandchildren.

Sylvia Michaels—A mother who has spent the past six months desperately searching for the baby stolen from her in Mexico.

Kacee Leblanc—Executive assistant with a shady past and shadier relatives who is in love with her boss, Tate Vincent.

Rosa Garcia—Former Austin City Police officer medically retired from the police force after receiving an injury in the line of duty. Tate Vincent hired her to protect his son.

El Corredor—Man in charge of trafficking babies in the San Antonio area and selling them to the highest bidders.

Danny Leblanc—Kacee's brother with a police record recently released from prison.

CW Middleton—Tate Vincent's ranch foreman and best friend. He served three tours of duty with the millionaire in the Middle East.

Jake Vincent—Tate Vincent's adopted son. Could he really be Sylvia's baby who disappeared six months ago?

Beth "Bunny" Kirksey—Woman claiming to be Jake's mother who signed over Jake to Tate in the adoption proceedings.

Velvet—Bunny's friend who may have information regarding the sale of babies in San Antonio.

Chapter One

Sylvia Michaels balanced tenuously on one long strand of barbed wire as she slung her leg over the fence. So far so good. Sweat dripped from her hairline, running down her forehead toward her eyes. No chance of brushing it away, not when she needed both hands to hold on.

Bowing her legs around the jagged barbs, she perched one foot on the wire and swung her other leg over. As she dropped to the ground, her jeans snagged on a sharp barb, ripping open the denim and tearing into her flesh. She screamed and fell the rest of the way, landing face-down on the ground, coughing up dust, bleeding and wishing this nightmare would end.

Overheated, tired and scared, she worried that this was just one more wild-goose chase she'd rack up on her quest to find her child. Adding to her stress, someone had been following her for the past couple days since she'd left the coroner's office in San Antonio. She choked not only on the fine Texas dirt, but a sob welled in her throat, despair threatening to take control.

Six months. She'd given up six months of her life to find the son stolen from her in Monterrey, Mexico, last March. He'd be ten months old now. She'd missed seeing him sit up for the first time, missed watching him learn to crawl. Possibly even missed his first word.

Damn it! She pushed to her feet, wiping the tears and dust from her eyes with her dirty hand. She hadn't come this far to fail. She hadn't risked her life investigating a potential baby-theft ring terrorizing mothers from Mexico to Texas. She'd been the only one to come forward and give a detailed description of the person who'd stolen her child. None of the other witnesses in Monterrey had seen the man's face or had the guts to identify the perpetrator if they had. She'd gone to the U.S. Embassy in Monterrey when the Mexican police had done nothing.

She should never have brought Jacob to visit her ex-husband. So what if his work made it impossible for him to travel to the States for his scheduled visit? She should have insisted he come to the States. And he'd blamed *her* when a man had knocked her down and taken Jacob from his stroller in broad daylight in a crowded marketplace.

After six months, a half dozen dead ends and completely draining her savings, she'd reached her limit, her last hope—the Vincent Ranch in Texas hill country. She'd followed every lead imaginable from a frightened Mexican woman who barely spoke English to an adoption agency in San Antonio. A child matching her son's description was adopted by Texas multimillionaire Tate Vincent two weeks after her son was abducted. When she'd tracked down the woman who'd signed over the child, she'd found she'd died in a hit-and-run the day before.

Sylvia had tried to get an appointment with Tate Vincent, but his personal assistant made excuses every time and flat-out told her to buzz off. It didn't help that she couldn't be openly honest with his assistant. What chance did she stand against a millionaire in claiming the son he'd adopted was in fact her son? She didn't have money left to fight a lengthy court battle to request an opportunity to even get close to the boy. All she had was the cash left in her wallet, beneath her car seat.

After all this time, Sylvia wanted desperately to see Jacob, to hold him in her arms, to hear his baby voice.

Sylvia had hidden her car a mile away behind brush, near a creek along the highway. She moved among the shadows to avoid detection, keeping close to a stand of dwarfed live oaks. A large field stretched in front of her, rising up a hillside with only scattered clumps of cedar and live oak. She hurried from shade patch to shade patch, sweat oozing from every pore.

When she'd left her car, her temperature gauge read ninety-eight. It felt more like well over one hundred. Her gaze darted from side to side, and she listened for sounds of people, horses or motor vehicles. As she topped the rise in the terrain, the Vincent Ranch house came into view, a large, sprawling, white limestone, one-story with a wraparound deck.

Her gaze panned the exterior, searching for movement. Careful to stay out of sight, she made a wide circle around the homestead until she rounded the front of the house. She paused in the shade of a tree, leaning against the gnarly trunk and squinting in the haze of dust and heat. Then she gasped, exhaustion, dehydration and hope bringing her to her knees.

There in the shadow of a large red oak stood a playpen. Leaning against one side was a baby tossing toys onto the grass. The wind ruffled the leaves on the shade tree, and a ray of sunlight found its way through the branches to the baby, gleaming off his head.

Sylvia clapped a hand to her mouth to keep from crying out. The baby had a cap of pale blond hair, highlighted by the sun's beam. It had to be Jacob. Her baby had spun-gold hair just like hers.

She staggered to her feet and pushed away from the tree, stumbling down the hillside toward the ranch house.

TATE VINCENT SLIPPED his right foot out of the stirrup and slid from the back of Diablo, his black quarterhorse stallion, one of the many horses he'd raised from a colt, since they could afford quality horses on the ranch. When his boots hit the dry Texas soil, a cloud of dust puffed up around him. "Need rain."

His foreman, C. W. Middleton, snorted. "Needed rain a month ago." He reached for Tate's reins, his own gelding tugging to get into the barn. "Let me take Diablo. I thought I heard Jake out in the yard. You go on—I'll manage the horses."

Tate grinned. "I'll take you up on that as soon as I get Diablo's saddle off. And remind me I owe you one."

"You don't owe me nothin'. You're the boss. I'm just hired help."

"Bull. We both know who runs this place." Tate followed C.W. into the cool shadows of the barn, tying Diablo to the outside of his stall. "You've been more than hired help since Dad died." He pulled at the thick leather strap, loosening the girth around Diablo's belly. When the strap dangled free, he lifted the saddle off the beast. The saddle blanket was drenched in sweat and coated in a heavy layer of fine Texas dust from their ride along the northern fence line. "Jake was asleep when we left this morning. I would like to see him again before he goes down for the night."

"Go on. Get out of here." Brush in hand, C.W. took over the care and grooming of Diablo, urging Tate out the door. "That boy thinks the sun rises and sets on you. 'Bout time you spent a little more daylight with him."

C.W. had been his friend since they'd met as army recruits. They'd gone on to Special Forces training and Afghanistan where they'd tracked down the al-Qaida rebels in the desert hills. Ranching in Texas seemed tame in comparison. But C.W. had fit right in, learning all the responsibilities of a good ranch hand. He'd learned how to ride, rope, brand and mend fences in a matter of weeks, too stubborn to admit defeat. Just like the boss. When the foreman had passed on, C.W. stepped up to the plate, assuming the role like he'd been born to do it.

Tate crossed the hard-packed ground between the barn and the Vincent homestead established by his great-great-grandfather in the mid-eighteen hundreds. He had to remind himself that he could hire people to do the work he did out in the field. The ranch wasn't what made him the money. His investments had taken him from struggling rancher to multimillionaire in just five years. Too bad his father hadn't lived longer to enjoy his son's success.

Richard Vincent had passed on five months earlier, his presence still missed by his son and the ranch staff. He hadn't gotten to know Jake a little better and Jake wouldn't know his grandfather.

Tate flexed his muscles, rolling the tension and weariness from his shoulders. Sure, he had the money to hire more ranch hands, but he liked the hard work. It kept him humble. At one point in his struggle to rise from rags to riches, he thought for sure he'd lose the ranch. He'd lost nearly everything else, including his wife.

Tate's mouth pressed into a thin line. Laura didn't have the stomach for the hard times. When cattle prices had plummeted and the creditors came knocking on their door, she'd packed up and left, stating that she'd only married him because she thought he was a wealthy land-owner. Not that he was sad to see her go. He was more upset at having wasted two years of his life on chasing her dreams instead of his own.

When he rounded the corner of the house, he spied a bright blue playpen situated in the shade with his son standing up against the inside of the pen. The child pushed a plush toy over the edge and watched it drop to the ground. Pickles, the black-and-white border collie, barely waited for it to leave Jake's hand before she grabbed it and shook it. Jake giggled and tried to get a leg up over the side of the pen. He liked playing with Pickles.

A swell of love and pride filled Tate's chest. Jake was his reason for living. He would never have thought he'd become so completely besotted over a kid. At the urging of his dying father, he'd arranged to adopt a baby boy. He'd paid big bucks to skip over the usual routine of social services snooping around his home, going directly to an adoption agency his executive assistant had located, one that specialized in quick adoptions. Pricey, but quick.

Now he couldn't put a price tag on what Jake brought to the Vincent household. Disappointed that Tate hadn't remarried and had a dozen grandchildren for him to spoil, Richard Vincent's dying wish was to hold his grandchild in his arms.

Tate stopped in front of the playpen.

When Jake saw him, his smile widened and he gurgled, reaching up with one hand.

"*Por favor,* don't pick him up, Señor Vincent." Rosa Garcia hurried forward, a frown on her pretty dark face. "*Usted está muy sucio.* Dirty. You are dirty."

"A little dirt never hurt a kid." Despite her admonishment, Tate lifted his son from the playpen and tossed him in the air.

Jake screamed and giggled, drool slipping from the side of his mouth to plop against Tate's shirt.

"Poor baby is still teething." Rosa reached out with a burp cloth to wipe up the drool.

Tate didn't care. He loved Jake more than anyone on God's green earth. Besides, a little spit was an improvement to his dust-caked clothing. "Hey, buddy. Have you and Pickles been playing fetch?"

"Da, da, da," Jake said.

Tate's eyes widened and a grin spread across his face. "Did you hear that? He just called me Dad."

Rosa's dark brown eyes rolled skyward. "He says that to me and *mi madré*."

Tate frowned. "Give a guy a break, will ya?" He tossed Jake into the air again, making the boy squeal with delight.

"Madré de Dios." Rosa hurried forward, reaching for Jake. "He just had a bottle of juice. Unless you want to wear the juice, don't shake him up so much."

Tate held Jake away from Rosa. "It's a little hot for him outside, isn't it?"

"We've only been out for *quince minutos.* Mama is cooking supper, Señorita Kacee drove to town to drop off papers at FedEx. *Por favor,* let me have Jake. You should shower before dinner is served."

Tate handed the child over to his caregiver, chucking him beneath his chin. "Okay, for now. I guess I am a little dirty."

Rosa plugged her nose, shaking her head. "Understatement." She balanced Jake on her hip and headed for the porch steps.

"Wait!" A shout from the field behind him made Tate turn.

A woman wearing jeans and a smudged white shirt—her hair flying out in long, blond strands—ran across the field, yelling, "Wait!"

Tate's brows dipped low. The fences along his property were posted with no trespassing signs. Only people with legitimate business were allowed access past the gate with clearance from his security service.

The woman's face was red and streaked with dirt and sweat. Her jeans were torn with blood staining the ragged edges, and she had a wild look in her eyes.

Tate shot a glance at Rosa. "Take Jake inside."

"Who do you think she is?" Rosa asked, clutching the baby to her chest.

"Do as I say," Tate bit out.

"*Sí,* Señor Vincent."

Rosa had been his buddy since childhood, having grown up on the Vincent Ranch alongside him. Why she insisted on calling him Señor Vincent was beyond him. With a wild woman crossing the field toward them, now wasn't the time to argue the point.

Rosa climbed the steps and hurried inside the house, Jake reaching over her shoulders, a wail rising from his little mouth.

"No! Please! Don't take him away!" The woman came to a halt at the wooden fence surrounding the yard. She grabbed the top rail and hauled herself up.

"Stop where you are." Tate didn't want her anywhere close to the house and his son. A crazy man who'd gotten past security had ultimately been the cause of his father's death five months ago. He refused to take any intrusion onto his property lightly. Without waiting for the woman to cross the fence, Tate marched across the manicured lawn.

Perched precariously on the top rail, the blonde swayed and fell over the fence, landing with a crash, her head hitting the post with a sharp crack.

When Tate reached her, she lay on the ground, her eyes staring up at the sky, blinking.

For a moment, Tate forgot to be angry with her.

Dirty and sweat-soaked, she was still a beautiful woman beneath the layer of smeared dust. When fat tears rolled out of the corners of her pale blue eyes, Tate couldn't help a sudden swell of protectiveness. He chalked it up to the fact that her eyes were the same pale blue as Jake's.

He dropped down beside her, forcing his voice to sound stern and distant when his instincts urged him to pick her up and carry her into his house. "Who the hell are you, and what are you doing on private property?"

She raised a hand to her head, and scraped it over her eyes. "Please. I only want to see him."

Tate's brows furrowed. "See who?"

"My son," she said, her voice wavering, dropping down to a whisper. Her eyes closed, and the woman had the nerve to pass out.

"Damned woman." His gut knotted and Tate swore. What did she mean by "my son"? He reached down and shook her. "Wake up."

She didn't budge.

He bent low, pressing his head to her chest to listen for breathing.

Although shallow, her breaths came regularly. Impatience gnawed at him. He couldn't shake her awake to answer his questions, and he couldn't really leave her out in the full force of the Texas sun. With his luck, her fall might have given her a concussion.

"Whatcha got there, boss?" C.W. trotted up beside him. When he got close enough to see the woman on the ground, he whistled. "Another stray?"

Tate glared at his foreman. "Looks like it."

"Want me to call the sheriff?"

"No." Why he didn't do just that, he couldn't explain. Something about the way she'd looked up at him, her gaze pleading with his, made him want to question her before he turned her over to the sheriff. Maybe she'd been mistaken, gotten the wrong place, hallucinated due to dehydration. She couldn't mean Jake. Jake couldn't be her son. He'd met Jake's mother. She'd signed the papers allowing him to adopt the boy. This woman was a stranger.

"If you're not going to call the sheriff, do you want me to call an ambulance?" C.W. rocked back on his boot heels. "Looks like she hit her head, and she's got a gash in her leg."

Tate's frown deepened. "No."

"Can't just leave her in the sun. She'll die of heat stroke."

He knew that, still he hesitated. "She's trespassing."

"Maybe so, but she is another human being. If you leave her here, you could be up on charges of negligent homicide."

If he took her into his house and she threatened his son, he'd be up on charges of murder anyway.

C.W. bent and reached for the woman.

"Don't." Tate held out his hand, blocking the man's attempt to lift her. "I'll get her." With all the trepidation of a man cornering a poisonous snake, Tate lifted the woman into his arms. Thin, light and limp, she had curves in all the right places and a soft pink mouth much too close to his own for him to think straight. What did she want? And why did he have this feeling that he wouldn't like what she had to say?

Morbid curiosity made him carry her into the cool air-conditioned interior of his home. He'd force-feed fluid into her and get her back on her feet, hear what she had to say and then send her packing. If that didn't work, then he'd call the sheriff and have her forcibly removed.

Rosa stood in the living room, Jake propped on her hip. "Who is she?"

"I don't know." Tate shot a pointed look at Jake's caregiver, a woman he'd hired not only for her skills with a child, but also for her skills as a bodyguard. A former Austin police officer, she had a proven track record taking out bad guys. "Take Jake to the nursery."

"But it's dinnertime."

"Feed him dinner in his room."

"Sí, Señor."

He laid the woman on the brown leather sofa in the living room.

Maria, Rosa's mother and also the housekeeper, entered through the doorway leading to the kitchen, carrying a damp rag and a glass of ice water.

Tate took the damp rag and laid it across the woman's forehead, mopping away a layer of dust and sweat. "Wake up, lady," he muttered, willing her eyes to open.

"Get her to drink," Maria urged.

Tate lifted the woman in one arm and touched the cool glass to her lips, letting the liquid slide down her throat.

At first the liquid filled her mouth and trickled out the sides. Then she swallowed and coughed, her eyes blinking open.

"What…" she said, her voice hoarse, her gaze blurred. "Are you—" she coughed again "—Tate Vincent?"

He frowned. She knew who he was, which meant she'd found her way to his place on purpose. Was she just another gold digger out to get money from him? "Yes," he answered, his tone clipped. "Who are you?"

Her eyes closed for a moment and then opened again. "I think you have my baby." After delivering that punch in the gut, the woman had the audacity to pass out again.

Chapter Two

Something blessedly cool stroked across Sylvia's forehead as she swam through the murkiness inside her head. A deep baritone hummed in the back of her mind, pulling her closer to the light. When the strokes moved to her cheek, she turned her face into the coolness and surfaced, her mind inching toward clarity. "Ummm, that feels good."

"Glad you think so. I'd appreciate it if you'd wake up before the sheriff arrives."

Sylvia's eyes popped open and she stared up into intense, brown eyes, so dark they could be considered black. A man with midnight-black hair and thick dark brows drawn into a frown glared down at her.

Fear and something else shot through her veins, pushing her to a sitting position. As soon as she sat up, her head swam and her world turned fuzzy around the edges. When she would have toppled over onto the floor, strong arms circled her shoulders and eased her back to cool leather.

"Who are you?" she asked as she edged one eye open and attempted a look around. All she could see was the broad chest and intimidating glare of the incredibly sexy man in front of her. He smelled of dust, sweat and leather. Very earthy and tremendously appealing.

"We'd already established the fact that I'm Tate Vincent. You're trespassing on my property." The man's countenance didn't change, except the glare deepened until his black eyes shot sparks. "Who the hell are you?"

She sighed, draping an arm over her brow to block out her unwanted attraction to the grouchy man. "Sylvia Michaels." As her vision cleared, so too did her memory. After a moment, she dropped her arm, her eyes widening. "You're Tate Vincent?" She sighed. "Oh, thank God."

"Don't be thanking Him yet. Give me one good reason why I shouldn't have you hauled off to jail for trespassing."

"I'm sorry. I tried to get an appointment to see you, but your assistant wouldn't give me one."

"That's why I have an assistant." His frown deepened, his face fierce. "Now that you have my attention, what exactly do you want?"

She stared up at him, her determination wavering briefly under his angry countenance. "I'm here because there's a good possibility that you have my child."

For a moment he said nothing, the only sign he had heard her was the muscle ticking dangerously in his jaw. "How much do you want?"

Sylvia's brow furrowed. "Want? What do you mean?"

"Most people who trespass or sneak onto my property want something, usually money. What's your price?"

Anger and indignation shot into her veins, stiffening her spine and forcing her back into an upright position. This time her vision didn't waver. "I don't want anything from you. I only want my child."

"And what makes you think I have him?"

Her eyes widened and a gasp whooshed from her lips.

"The baby I saw outside is a boy?" Joy filled her chest. "I knew it," she said, her happiness stealing breath from her lungs. "How is he? Where is he?" She leaned to the side to look around Tate.

Strong fingers gripped her arms, forcing her to look at him. "I don't know what kind of game you're playing, but I don't have your son."

She took a deep, steadying breath. "Did you adopt a child about six months ago?"

"Anyone who follows the gossip columns would know the answer to that." The muscle ticked in his jaw again. "Besides, it's none of your business."

If she wasn't mistaken, she'd scored a hit and she wasn't backing off until she got answers. She stared up at him, her mouth firming into a determined line. "It is my business if that child was stolen from me."

"You're wrong. I met the mother of my son. She signed the papers in front of an attorney swearing the child was hers and that she was giving away all legal rights to him."

"Was her name Beth Kirksey?"

Tate's eyes narrowed. "And if it was?"

"She wasn't the mother of the baby you adopted. The birth certificate was forged. She'd given up her real baby for adoption four months earlier. The baby she gave you was mine."

"I don't believe you." He reached for the cell phone in his back pocket. "A quick call will confirm."

"Don't bother, Ms. Kirksey won't be answering."

"Why?"

"She's dead." Sylvia swallowed hard. "She was killed in a hit-and-run 'accident' a week ago."

"I'm calling the sheriff." He stood, towering above her. If he'd intimidated her before, he terrified her now.

Well over six feet tall, his massive presence and his ferocious scowl could stop an angry bull in his tracks.

But Sylvia hadn't come this far or risked this much to give up now. "Just let me see him. Please."

"No way. For all I know, you're crazy and might hurt my son. You'd do well to get the hell out of my house now while I'm feeling generous enough to let you go without a police escort."

Sylvia crossed her arms over her chest. "I'm not leaving until I see my son."

"We'll see about that." He nodded to the man standing in the doorway. "C.W., call the sheriff."

"Will do, boss."

"Wait." Sylvia couldn't afford to waste time in jail. She had to see her son. "I can prove he's my son."

"Yeah, and I'm the King of Hearts." Tate turned away. "I don't have time for this nonsense. Keep an eye on her, will you, C.W.?"

Sylvia rose from the couch, swaying but determined, and reached for his arm before he could walk away. "He has blond hair and blue eyes just like mine, doesn't he?"

"So what if he does? His mother had blond hair and blue eyes."

"Does your son have a star-shaped strawberry birthmark on his right hip?"

About to take a step, the man stopped in midstride, his back to her, his body rigid. "That proves nothing."

Her hand tightened on his arm, her nails digging in. Then she let go, her fingers going to her waistband. She loosened the button of her jeans and unzipped the fly. Then with a deep breath, she shoved the jeans down low enough to expose her right hip. "Does it look like this?"

The man Tate had called C.W. stopped in the doorway and let out a long, low wolf whistle.

Tate's chest expanded and contracted before he finally stared down at the mark on her hip. "How do I know that's real?"

"Touch it," she said, her voice catching in her throat. The thought of the big cowboy touching her made her tingle all over, but she held steady. She had to do this to get her son back.

His hand came out and he rubbed a work-roughened thumb across the birthmark. "It could be a tattoo."

Sylvia's breath caught in her chest and she held it for a moment before replying, electric current tingling throughout her body from where his fingers touched her. "You know it's not. It's as real as the one on my son's hip." She pulled her jeans up and zipped. "Can I see him now?"

His mouth drew into a tight, forbidding line. Then he caught her by her arms and shook her. "Get it through your head, he's not your son! Now, get out of my house." He practically flung her away from him.

Steadying herself against the back of the couch, Sylvia struggled to remain calm. Even with Tate breathing fire down on her, she refused to give up. "Not without my son."

"You won't see him without a court order. I'll be contacting my lawyer. I suggest you contact yours."

Sylvia's heart dropped to her stomach. She didn't have a nickel left in her account and she'd been living on credit cards for the past month until they had maxed out. A long court battle would be way out of her league. She flung her long hair back and stood with her shoulders squared, her feet wide, hands propped on her hips. All she had left was false bravado and her conviction that she'd really found her son. "If you want me to leave, you'll have to call the sheriff. I'm not going anywhere until I see my son."

"Let me remind you who is trespassing and who is within legal rights to shoot you."

"Wouldn't be the first time I've been shot at trying to find my son. Go ahead." Inside she shook, but she refused to show him an ounce of fear. "I want to see the son stolen from me in Mexico six months ago."

"What's it going to take to convince you that he's not your son?"

"Show me his right hip. If the birthmark isn't there, I'll leave, no argument." Sylvia held her chin high and when her mouth threatened to tremble, she bit down hard on her lower lip.

Tate sucked in a deep breath and let it out. It did nothing to calm the racing beat of his heart. He sucked in another breath and tried again. But as long as the woman who claimed to be his son's mother stood in his living room, he couldn't get enough air into his lungs.

After all the years he'd begged Laura for children… then she'd left and his father had died. Tate refused to give up the only family he had left. Ever since he'd adopted Jake, he'd had that niggling worry in the back of his mind that someone would someday come and claim him. Hadn't he seen court cases where the mother came back and claimed she'd been wrong to let her child go? Never afraid of anything in his life, Tate feared losing Jake. He stiffened.

No way in hell.

"C.W., help me load this woman into the truck so we can kick her off the ranch."

C.W.'s lips curled upward. "Gladly." As he walked toward Sylvia, his grin widened. "If you don't mind me saying, I wish it had been me touching that birthmark, ma'am."

Sylvia raised her fists to a fighting position and squared off with C.W. "Touch me, and I'll break every one of your fingers. I won't leave until I see my son."

Tate shook his head. "Lady, I don't know what happened to *your* son, but since you're not going to see *my* son, you might as well shove off."

The front door to the house slammed open. "Tate?" Kacee LeBlanc's heels clicked across the hardwood floors in double time. "What's with the fire down by the creek?" She jerked to a halt when she spied Sylvia with her fists up. "Who the hell's she?"

Tate nodded toward Sylvia. "This woman claims to be Jake's mother."

"That's just bull. I was there when the real birth mother signed over the child. She didn't look anything like this woman. Other than the blond hair." Kacee whipped out her cell phone. "Have you called the sheriff?"

"We were just about to do that." Tate stared pointedly at Sylvia. "Care to leave before he gets here?"

"You call him Jake?" Sylvia smiled. "My son's name is Jacob."

"I don't care what *your* son's name is. He's *my* son."

"I'm not budging until I see the baby."

"Oh, you'll be budging all right." Tate nodded to Kacee. "Make that call."

She punched a button on her cell phone. While she waited for an answer, she frowned. "There's a fire down by the creek. You might want to get some of the ranch hands on it before it spreads."

"Fire?" C.W.'s brows rose. "Damn, as dry as it is, it'll spread fast." He nodded at Tate. "You can handle her on your own?"

"Go. We can't afford a range fire. Take Dalton, Cody and anyone else who's back from the south range."

"Will do." C.W. ran out of the room.

"Yes, we have an emergency. This is Kacee LeBlanc out at the Vincent Ranch. We have a fire by the highway near Rocky Creek. We also have a trespasser at the ranch house." Kacee's steel-gray gaze scraped Sylvia from head to toe. "Send the sheriff. The woman claims to be Jake's mother and refuses to leave. Thirty? That's the best he can do? Okay. Thank you." She flipped her cell phone shut and tilted her head to the side. "The sheriff will be here soon." She crossed the room to Tate and touched his arm. "Want me to get a gun, Tate? You know you can shoot trespassers, especially if they're threatening you or a loved one." Her voice was hard, her words menacing. She meant to scare the woman across the room, dressed in a dirty shirt and jeans, looking like she'd been run through the wringer of his grandmother's old-timey washing machine.

Despite her threat to his son, Tate didn't like where Kacee was going. "No. I reckon she's harmless."

Kacee leaned in to whisper, her breath warm on his ear. "That's what you thought about that homeless man who stabbed your father."

A band tightened around Tate's chest. "That's enough, Kacee." But he wasn't taking any chances. He walked to the desk in the far corner of the room, removed a gun from the drawer and dropped the clip from the chamber. From another drawer he retrieved bullets, sliding them into the clip. "But it doesn't hurt to be cautious."

"Good grief. I'm not here to hurt anyone. I only want my son." Sylvia Michaels, eyes wide and face pale, backed toward the door, her hands raised.

"Take one more step, and I'll shoot," Tate warned.

She paused for only a moment, her gaze connecting with his, determination hardening her chin. Then she spun around, throwing her parting comment over her shoulder. "Then just shoot me."

Chapter Three

With a gun pointed at her back, Sylvia's skin crawled, but she pushed forward, headed for a hallway and the sound of a baby squealing happily.

"Damned woman." The cowboy cursed behind her, his boots clattering against the wooden flooring.

"Give me the gun, Tate. I'll shoot her," the woman Sylvia assumed was the assistant called out.

If Sylvia had any chance at all of seeing Jacob, she'd have to move faster than the two people behind her. She shot away from the man holding the gun, her heart pounding in her chest. Several doors opened off the hallway, only one remained closed and the joyous sounds of a baby could be heard through the wood paneling. Without slowing, she grabbed the handle and opened the door.

A large hand clamped down so hard on her shoulder she jerked to a halt, unable to move another step.

She caught a glimpse of a baby boy sitting in a high chair, a cracker clutched in his fist. All she got was that little peek before Tate Vincent flung her around and shoved her against the hallway wall. "You hurt one hair on my son's head and I'll kill you."

With the door wide-open, the sounds of the baby's cooing reached her, warmth spreading throughout her body, filling all the cold, empty places she'd endured since Jacob had been stolen away from her in Mexico. Tears welled in her eyes, blurring her vision. "Please." She sniffed, unashamed of begging for a chance to see her son. "Please. I want to see him. If he's not mine, I'll leave."

For a long moment, the man glared down at her, his heavy hand never leaving her shoulder. Based on his size, he'd probably be ten times stronger than her. More than Sylvia could hope to fight off, but she would do anything to see Jacob again.

"You say your son was abducted six months ago. How will you recognize him besides the birthmark? Babies change a lot in six months."

"I'll know," she said. Didn't mothers always know the cries of their own babies? After six months of searching, she'd almost given up hope. Could this cowboy be right? Would she recognize her son? Her shoulders pushed back and she wiped the tears from her eyes with an angry hand. "I'll know."

Another long moment passed, Tate's eyes narrowing into slits. "How do I know you're not here to hurt him?"

"Oh, God." A nervous, almost hysterical laugh escaped her lips. "I wouldn't hurt my own son. I've spent the past six months looking for him, hoping no one has hurt him. I just want to see him. That's all I ask." She'd work on custody once she was satisfied the baby truly was Jacob. "Don't you see? You could be just as much a victim as I am. My baby was stolen. Your baby could have been signed over to you illegally."

"I met the mother, she signed the papers, I adopted him. My lawyer went over the paperwork at least a dozen times."

"Still, you could have been duped. The baby may not have been that woman's to give."

He smacked the hand holding the gun flat against the wall. "The contract was ironclad. You're a liar!"

Sylvia winced, but stared up at him, meeting his glare with a level stare. "I don't lie."

"And if my son has this birthmark, that doesn't prove anything."

"Maybe not. If the birthmark is there, then we do a DNA test." How she'd come up with the money, she didn't know, but she'd get her baby back if she had to sell her soul to the devil himself.

The baby giggled in the next room, so joyous and innocent.

All the motherly longing she'd buried deep inside surged into her chest, squeezing her lungs so hard she couldn't breathe. "Just let me see him."

The man's eyes narrowed even more. "I don't trust you."

"Search me. I'm not carrying any weapons. I only want to see if he has the birthmark. I won't try to take him away. I won't hurt him." Her voice caught on a sob, rising up to choke her. "I need to know."

"You're not buying this crap are you?" The woman in the business suit stood with her hands held out in front of her, a small pistol clutched between her fingers.

Tate Vincent shot a stern look at her. "Put the gun down, Kacee."

The beautiful assistant pouted. "You take away all my fun."

"Put it down." Tate stared at Sylvia, his words directed at Kacee. "I can handle this. I don't want my son injured by a stray bullet."

The other woman's hand lowered. "Good point. Besides, the sheriff should be here any moment."

"Why don't you go watch for him."

Kacee frowned. "But, what if…"

"Just go," Tate bit out. "I can handle this." He stared down at Sylvia, his steely brown-eyed gaze boring into her. When Kacee rounded the corner, he growled, "Why should I believe any of this?"

Tired, dizzy and beyond her endurance, Sylvia stared back at the millionaire who could have had her physically removed by now, but for some unknown reason hadn't. "If you had your child stolen from you, would you just let him go?"

The man holding her arm continued to glare, the silence lengthening between them. When Sylvia thought he wouldn't respond to her question, the man sighed, his grip loosening. "No, I would never stop looking."

"Exactly." Hope blossomed in her chest, a smile trembling on her lips. "Then you'll let me see him?"

His hold stiffened. "I didn't say that."

She raised her hand to peel his fingers loose from her arm. "Please. I've been searching for so long. If there is any chance the baby in there is mine…"

For a brief moment, Tate's face grew haggard, then his mouth tightened, the expression returning to the cold hard mask of a harsh businessman. "Are you prepared if the boy isn't yours?"

"If he has the birthmark—"

"I repeat, the birthmark proves nothing." Tate's hand squeezed tighter. She'd have a bruise there by morning.

"If he has the birthmark, will you agree to a DNA test?" To be this close was killing her. "Look, I know this can't be easy for you, either. You've had Jacob for

the past six months. I only had him for four." She gave
a watery smile. "But I remember what a good baby he
was, always laughing and happy. If he's like he was back
then, anyone would fall in love with the little guy. His
smile could light up a room."

"I'm going to let you go. Don't try anything." Tate's
hand loosened and dropped to his side.

Sylvia closed her eyes and sent a silent prayer to the
heavens. Then she opened them again. "Then, you'll let
me see him?"

"On one condition."

"Name it."

"You can't touch him. I don't want you anywhere close
to my son."

Sylvia dragged in a deep breath and let it go. Her arms
ached with the need to hold her son, but she could wait
a little bit longer. She swallowed hard. "Okay."

Tate sensed that by showing the woman his son everything would change. But the look in her eyes, the desperate plea to see the boy tugged at Tate's heart. This dusty
woman who'd defied his no trespassing signs, crossed
long distances, chased leads and finally made it to his
home showed a courage he hadn't seen in the women
he'd known. *If* everything she said was true. Not that he
believed any of it, yet.

The thought of having Jake stolen from him made his
stomach clench into a bigger knot than he could have
imagined.

"Señor Vincent?" Rosa, clutching Jake against her
chest, peered around the door. "Is everything okay?"

The golden-haired child spied him, squealed and
reached out for Tate. Instinctively, he held out his arms
for his son. Jake fell into them, giggling.

Over the top of his son's golden head, Tate could see

the trespasser's eyes fill with tears, spilling over and running down her cheeks. Her hand rose as if to touch Jake.

Tate stepped back, out of reach.

Her hand fell to her side. "Will you look?" she whispered.

He told himself it didn't matter if his son had the star-shaped birthmark. Nothing short of a DNA test would convince him. But the pale blue of his son's gaze reflected through the sheen of tears in the woman's eyes. The bright gold cap of silky smooth hair resembled that of the woman with the long, straight, blond locks.

"Please," she said, her voice a quiet entreaty in the hallway.

His heart heavy, Tate pulled the tape tab from the right side of Jake's disposable diaper and pushed the plastic and cotton aside.

There on his right hip was a light red birthmark in the shape of a star.

Sylvia gasped. "Oh, God, oh, God...I've found him." Then she sank to the floor, burying her head in her hands, silent sobs shaking her narrow frame.

"Tate, the sheriff's here." Kacee's heels clicked a sharp staccato on the smooth, Mexican terra-cotta tiles. "He wants to talk to you. I told him about her." His assistant's brows rose as her gaze found Sylvia on the floor. "Good Lord, did she pass out again?"

"Rosa, take Jake to the kitchen and let him finish his meal there." Tate handed his son to his caregiver and squatted beside the overcome interloper. "You come with me." He held out his hand.

When she placed her hand in his, he couldn't ignore the spark of electricity, the flare of desire he'd felt. She was just a crazy woman out to take his son away from him. Most likely, she was after more. Maybe she wanted to blackmail him.

But the watery blue eyes staring up at him were just like Jake's and had a similar melting quality that affected him more than he'd likely admit. Angry with himself for feeling anything for this person who claimed Jake was hers, who threatened to take away the only family Tate had left, he jerked her up off the floor.

Sylvia came up so fast, she slammed into his chest. His arm came up around her narrow waist, steadying her against him.

Her breath caught on a gasp, her fingers laying flat against his shirt, her eyes wide. "I…I can stand on my own." She gave a light push to free herself.

"Sure you can." For some reason he couldn't let go, his arm slipping around her waist. Mistake, his brain warned. "You've already fainted once. I refuse to give you another opportunity to bring a lawsuit against me." The lawsuit of his life loomed like a dark cloud of doom. If Jake truly was her child, he'd be in a hellacious court fight like no other.

He steered her toward the living room. Her gaze darted toward the kitchen doorway as they passed, Jake's giggles carrying through. "I've found him," she whispered, a smile curving her lips.

"Don't count your chickens, lady," Tate grumbled. "You're trespassing on private property."

Sheriff Thompson stood in the living room, his hat in his hand. "Mr. Vincent." He nodded.

"Sheriff." Tate guided Sylvia to a seat and pressed her into it.

"Ms. LeBlanc tells me you have a trespasser." He tipped his head toward Sylvia. "This the one?"

Tate didn't look at Sylvia. "Yes."

The woman in question gasped. "I only wanted to see my child. How can that be a crime?"

"You want to file charges, Mr. Vincent?" Sheriff Thompson crossed the living room and stood in front of Sylvia, his feet parted, his hands fiddling with the case containing the handcuffs attached to his utility belt.

The blonde stared across at Tate, that same desperation in her eyes gnawing away at the knot in his gut. Damn it! He didn't need this. "No," he said.

"Are you crazy?" Kacee marched over to him and laid a hand on his arm. "Remember what happened to your father? Are you willing to let something like that happen to Jake?"

Tate finally turned and stared into Sylvia's eyes. "I really don't think she'll hurt Jake."

"You willing to bet Jake's life on that?" Kacee planted hands on her hips. When Tate refused to meet her eyes, his gaze still on Sylvia, Kacee threw her hands in the air. "Don't get mad when I tell you I told you so."

Sylvia stood, her mouth pressed into a thin line. "If you don't feel comfortable my being around Jacob, I'll leave with the sheriff. But I promise I'll be back for my son."

Tate's gaze nailed hers. "For the moment, she can stay."

Sheriff Thompson shrugged. "Okay, then maybe you can tell me whose car it is burned up in the creek outside your property?"

Sylvia's gaze shifted to the sheriff. "A car in the creek? Was it a Ford Escort?"

The sheriff's eyes narrowed. "Yes, ma'am."

"That's my car!" Sylvia's hand rose to her mouth.

"Sorry, lady. It's totaled. Looks like someone didn't like where you parked."

"What do you mean?"

The sheriff shook his head, his mouth a thin line. "Someone lit a rag and stuffed it in the gas tank. By the time we got to it, it was already history."

Chapter Four

Sylvia sank onto the couch, suddenly light-headed. "That's all I had left," she whispered. Worse, it confirmed her worst fears. Someone had been following her since she'd left San Antonio. Burning her car had been a message.

Dear God, the car had been her home for the past few weeks. She'd let her apartment go, sold her furniture and everything else to allow her to continue her search. Now that she'd found Jacob...what next?

How could she start over when she didn't have enough money in her bank account for a cup of coffee and all her credit cards were maxed out? She didn't have enough money to hire a cab to take her back to town, much less hire a lawyer to sue for custody. Despair, fear, joy, the emotions drained every last bit of fight left in her.

No car and no money meant she'd never get her child back. Even if she did, would she provide a safe home for him? Who was after her? What did he want? Why burn her car? Her head spun with the unending barrage of questions.

Then she heard a child's happy squeal echoing against the walls. Her back stiffened and she forced herself to a standing position, facing the sheriff. "That was my car, Sheriff."

"Since it appears to be arson, we have to have it towed to the impound lot for a thorough investigation. I'll need a statement from both you and Mr. Vincent, seeing as how the car was found in the creek, which is part of Mr. Vincent's property."

"Were there any tracks or clues as to who might have done it?" Tate asked.

Sheriff Thompson shook his head. "I arrived just minutes before the pump truck. They sucked every last drop of their tank dry putting out the fire and tamping down the dry brush around the site. Nothing left but mud and ashes." He turned to Sylvia. "Why did you park in the creek anyway, Ms....?"

"Michaels, Sylvia Michaels." Sylvia swallowed and looked down at her dirty hands. "I needed to see Mr. Vincent." She glanced up, her gaze clashing with Tate's.

His brown eyes narrowed and he shook his head slightly, almost imperceptibly.

Sylvia turned toward the sheriff. "On a personal matter."

"So you trespassed." Sheriff Thompson's brows rose. "You sure you didn't light the fire in the car yourself?"

"No, sir." Nor could she tell either of the men that she thought she was in danger. What court in the land would give her custody of any child if they thought her unfit to provide a safe haven for him?

"Really, Tate, you trust this woman in your home? She just admitted to hiding her car so that she could get in to see you?" Kacee rolled her eyes. "If that isn't crazy, I don't know what is."

"It's up to you, Mr. Vincent. I'm headed back to town. I can take her with me. Just say the word."

Tate Vincent stared at Sylvia for a long, drawn-out moment.

Her heart hammered blood through her veins, pounding against her eardrums, but she refused to look away from his intense gaze. She pushed her shoulders back and her chin tipped upward just slightly. If she had to, she'd beg to stay. But for now, he needed to know she wasn't backing down.

"She can stay." His eyes narrowed even more. "For now."

Kacee snorted. "Tate, be reasonable."

"Thank you, Sheriff Thompson. Let us know what you find out about the car." Tate walked toward the front entrance, opened the door and held it for the sheriff.

The sheriff gave Sylvia one last look, plunked his hat on his head and took the hint. "I'll be in touch."

Once the sheriff had descended the stairs and climbed into his SUV with the word *sheriff* marked in bold letters on both sides, Tate let the screen door swing shut.

Sylvia braced herself for the storm to come.

"What are you going to do with her now?" Kacee asked, her high-heeled foot tapping against the wooden floor.

"On your way home, contact Dr. Richards. Tell him I want a DNA sampling kit out here ASAP."

Kacee flipped her phone open. "I'll just call him, now."

Tate glared at her. "Do it on your way out, Kacee. I don't need your services for the rest of the afternoon."

"But—"

The man stopped her next words with the look on his face.

Sylvia almost felt sorry for the woman, except for the fact she would have happily shot her for trespassing. Once the millionaire's assistant left, Sylvia would be alone with Tate Vincent. In his current mood, the meeting wouldn't be pleasant. But at least she could speak plainly when they were alone.

She'd let him know she'd fight with every last breath to get her son back. But she wouldn't tell him her breath and the clothes on her back were all she had left to her name.

Tate stood at the door, holding it open much as he'd done for the sheriff. Kacee pouted, her brows drawing together as she gathered her briefcase and car keys. "We haven't gone over the figures on the purchase of the Double Diamond Ranch."

"Tomorrow." He held the door and waved his hand, inviting her through.

Kacee sucked in a deep breath and blew it out, crossing the threshold as directed. When she passed by Tate, she leaned close to him. "She's nothing but trouble, I tell you."

"I can handle it."

"I know...without me." She glared over her shoulder at Sylvia.

Tate shut the door behind Kacee and stared after her as she climbed into her car and drove away. Not until her dust trail cleared the driveway did he drag in a deep breath and turn to Sylvia standing quietly behind him.

"You know I'm telling the truth, don't you?" Sylvia whispered. "You know Jacob is my son."

Anger bolted through him. "No, I don't know anything." But that niggle of doubt made him more afraid than any other time in his life. Losing Jake ranked right up there with losing his father. Jake was family. He couldn't lose him. "What other proof do you have that you ever had a child?"

Sylvia reached into the back pocket of her jeans and pulled out a crumpled piece of paper and a tattered photograph. "His birth certificate and a photograph of him when he was four months old." Her lips twisted in a semblance of a smile and she shook her head. "They are the only things I have left of Jacob. Everything else was in my car." Tears filled her eyes, making them a shimmering blue, so like Jake's when he didn't want to lie down for his nap.

Rosa always told Tate to let Jake cry himself to sleep, let him learn to soothe himself. But Tate couldn't, not when the child looked up at him through those liquid blue eyes. He wanted to hold him, make the fear go away, make him know that nothing on the earth would take this child away from him.

Tate's fists tightened and he resisted the draw of Sylvia's blue, watery eyes. He snatched the paper and the photograph from her hands. Prolonging the inevitable, he bent to read the words on the document, etched in permanent ink with the state seal of Texas embossing the corner.

Mother's Maiden Name: Sylvia Leigh Michaels. Father: Miguel Tikas. Baby's Name: Jacob Paul Michaels. The birth date indicated ten months ago.

Ignoring the knot twisting in his gut, Tate handed the paper back to Sylvia, telling himself it was just a piece of paper. It didn't prove anything. Then he stared down at the picture of a baby with golden hair and bright blue eyes. The baby could be Jake six months ago. He had the same smile, the same halo of golden hair. Damn it! Jake was his son!

He clutched the photograph in his hand, his gaze rising to lock with the woman in front of him. "How do I know you really are Sylvia Michaels? That you aren't lying and that you didn't steal this document?"

The dusty blonde fished in her back pocket, pulled

out a card and handed it to him. He stared down at the hard plastic of a Texas driver's license. An image of a blond woman smiled up at him. Less gaunt, her hair neatly combed into long, straight lengths, she looked happy, healthy and different than the woman standing in his living room. But the resemblance was there. On the license, the name read Sylvia Leigh Michaels, just like on the birth certificate. The address that of San Antonio, Texas.

Again, Tate forced himself to remain calm. This was all just a bad dream. He inhaled a full, deep breath and let it out slowly, handing the card back to Sylvia, his hand still curled around the photograph. "What do you want from me?"

She folded the driver's license into the birth certificate and shoved them into her back pocket. "I only want my son." She held out her palm. "May I have my picture back? It's the only one I have left."

Strangely reluctant, he handed her the photo, their fingers touching briefly, the impact sending a jolt of something he couldn't describe through his veins.

"So what now?" she asked.

"I won't let Jake go without a fight."

"Then you admit there might be truth in what I say?"

"You present a good argument, but anyone can forge documents. You could have had a child. There's no guarantee my son is the son you had stolen."

"But you agree that there is a possibility that someone might have forged the birth certificate you have?"

"I'm not agreeing to anything until I have my lawyer check into it."

Sylvia nodded, her shoulders rising and falling on a

sigh. "I didn't expect you'd give up without a fight. But I'm not, either."

"Please leave. My lawyer will be in touch with yours." He moved toward the front door, holding it open. "And I need to know where you will be staying."

Sylvia stared across at him, her lower lip caught between her teeth. That little display of uncertainty doing funny things to him. She didn't answer.

"I'll need an address to forward any documents from my legal staff."

"I don't have an address."

Tate shook his head. "What do you mean you don't have an address? Don't you live in San Antonio?"

"I did. I don't. Oh, hell." She threw her hands in the air. "I haven't lived anywhere but hotels and my car since Jacob was stolen. I let my apartment go."

"I'll have my foreman drop you at the hotel in Canyon Springs."

"Wouldn't do much good," she muttered, refusing to meet his gaze.

"What did you say?" Tate asked.

"Nothing. Never mind. I'll accept that ride since my car is toast."

"Answer me first. What did you say?"

When she stood in stony silence, refusing to answer him, Tate grabbed her shoulders. "You try my patience, woman. You've barged into my life, threatening to take my son from me, the least you can do is answer my question."

Sylvia threw off his hands, dull red spreading up her neck into her cheeks, her eyes flashing. "I don't have anywhere to go. Everything I owned went up in flames in my car. What little money I had left with it. I'm broke,

I'm homeless and I'm tired of you yelling at me! All I want is my son back."

Her hand lifted to her mouth, her eyes widening. "Don't think lack of money will stop me from getting Jacob back. I can provide him a good stable home. I can. No judge or jury in the state of Texas will deny my right to Jacob. He's my son!"

She stood trembling, her fists clenched at her sides, her blue eyes turning stormy.

If Tate wasn't facing losing Jake, he'd find her defiance attractive, her flashing blue eyes beautiful and the tilt of her breasts appealing. But damn it, she wanted to take his son away from him. "You'll stay here for now."

Sylvia gasped. "What did you say?"

"You heard me. Now don't make me change my mind."

"I can't stay here."

"Take it or leave it." He walked to the edge of the room and leaned out into the hallway. "Maria!"

"But…" Sylvia's brow creased, her head tipped to the side. "But I want to take Jacob away from you. Why would you do this?"

"Maria!"

"Sí, Señor." The older Hispanic woman hurried toward Tate, breathing hard, her forehead knitted in a concerned frown.

"Prepare a room for Ms. Michaels."

Her brows rose into her graying hair. *"Porqué?"*

"She'll be staying here." Tate frowned. "Now, please prepare the room."

"Sí." Maria shot another confused stare at Sylvia and turned away.

"Get this straight…" Tate directed his attention to

Sylvia. "I'll be watching you. If you attempt to take Jake before any of this mess is legally settled, I'll kill you."

Sylvia's hand went to her throat, her face blanching. "How do I know you won't try to kill me anyway?"

"All you have is my word."

"I don't know you, Mr. Vincent. Is your word enough to go on?"

"You're asking me to go on your word that Jake is your son." He gave her a challenging look, all the while wondering what he was getting himself into.

"But you should hate me," Sylvia whispered. She didn't think he'd heard until he turned back to her with a pointed gaze.

"I have a philosophy of keeping my friends close, and my enemies closer."

Chapter Five

Sylvia stood at the window of the spacious bedroom, staring out at the dry Texas hill country, her gaze panning the horizon but not seeing a thing. Her ears perked at every sound in the household, hoping to hear the faint noises a baby makes. Her baby. Jacob.

So tuned in to the specific sounds of a child, she didn't hear adult footsteps outside her door.

"These should fit you."

Sylvia spun, her hand going to her throat. "Oh, Lord, you scared me."

The young Hispanic woman Tate had called Rosa, the woman who'd been caring for Jacob in the nursery, stepped into the room, moving with a slight limp. She laid a stack of clothing on the bed, the corner of her lips quirking upward. "These belonged to Mr. Vincent's ex. I found them in a bag of clothing *mi madré* planned to donate to the homeless shelter. That and an old Mexican dress my mother wore." Rosa's lip curled tighter into a sneer.

Sylvia had read everything she could find in the San Antonio public library about the infamous young millionaire and most eligible bachelor of the state of Texas. His wife had walked out on him early in their marriage when Tate wasn't so rich. In fact, he'd been close to losing his ranch and everything he owned when his wife walked out on him. Had she stuck with him "for richer or poorer" she'd have been sitting pretty in this fabulous house that Tate had built onto and modernized to make it anyone's dream home, not wanting for anything. Stupid woman.

Feeling every bit the homeless person, Sylvia had no other choice but to take what was offered, even if it had been the ex-wife's clothing. Another possible strike against her in her struggle to get her child back—a reminder to the great Tate Vincent of what he'd lost in his failed marriage. "Thank you."

"Don't thank me. Mr. Vincent is to thank for allowing you to stay." Rosa's eyes narrowed. "Just so you know, I'm Jake's nanny…and bodyguard. I'm expert with the nine millimeter and I've never missed a target."

A shiver snaked up the back of Sylvia's neck. Jacob's bodyguard could no doubt take her, but Sylvia had no intention of letting Rosa know she was scared. Her back straightened and she tipped her head back, her brows rising. "Are you threatening me?"

Rosa shrugged. "All I'm saying is that the Vincents—that would be Tate and Jake—are like family to me. Hurt either one of them and…" She stared straight into Sylvia's gaze. "Let's just say, a nine-millimeter bullet can make a pretty big mess."

Before Sylvia could respond, the Hispanic woman turned and limped away.

The image she'd left Sylvia with was of herself being gunned down by a crazy woman with a pistol. "And this is the woman he trusts with my son?" Sylvia muttered, her hand sifting through the clothing on the bed. "Maybe I should check for explosive devices before I wear any of this."

"I see you've met Rosa."

Sylvia squealed and dropped the shirt she'd lifted from the pile, her face burning.

The man who'd been with Tate when he'd found her in the pasture stood with his hat in his hand. "Yes, Rosa can be pretty harsh with her words, but she wouldn't hide explosives in clothing. She's more…" The man paused, his hands turning the hat in his fingers before he stopped and looked up. "She's more in-your-face violent. You'll know when she plans to do harm."

"That's supposed to make me feel better?"

He shrugged. "Don't take her too seriously. She's had a bug up her…" Color rose in the man's cheeks, making them a ruddy-brown. "Well, since she took a bullet in Austin." A brief shadow crossed his face, then he smiled, his deeply tanned skin crinkling at the corners of his eyes. "I'm C.W., the foreman. Supper's ready."

Sylvia's stomach growled. She wanted to say that she wasn't hungry. The truth was she hadn't eaten since last night when she'd left the library in San Antonio to drive here. "Thank you."

C.W. waited for Sylvia to pass through the door. "About what Rosie said—"

"Don't call me Rosie. I hate it when you call me Rosie." Rosa's voice called out from another room down the hallway.

C.W. chuckled and winked. "Love to get her goat." All humor left his face. "As for what Rosie—Rosa—said… Same goes for me. Tate and Jake mean the world to all of us. If anything happens…"

Although C.W. said the words gently, Sylvia couldn't mistake the steel behind them. "You have a nine-milli-meter bullet with my name on it, right?"

He nodded. "Something like that."

"Point taken." Sylvia sighed. "I'm not here to hurt

either one of them. I'm here to get my son back. My son. The child I gave birth to and didn't willingly give up." She planted her fists on her hips and squared off with C.W. "Did you hear that, Rosa?" she called out loud enough for the woman down the hallway to hear.

"Sí." Rosa stepped through a doorway, Jacob perched in her arms, his baby fists waving and a wet smile spreading across his chubby cheeks at the sight of C.W. "Let the courts decide where Jake belongs."

Sylvia's heart melted at the sight of her son.

C.W. met Rosa halfway down the hallway, reaching for the child. "Come here, little man. Come see ol' Uncle C.W."

Ready tears sprang to Sylvia's eyes. Jacob was beautiful. He'd grown into a healthy, happy baby. At least she could rest assured he hadn't been abused since coming to the Vincent Ranch. All those months of worry could be left behind. When Jacob had been stolen, Sylvia imagined all kinds of horrors her son could have been subjected to. She'd cried too many tears thinking about it.

The smile on Jacob's face, the happiness he displayed for the people surrounding him let Sylvia know that he'd found a loving family to take care of him until his own mother could find him.

Her arms ached to reach out and hold her son, but she held back, determined to let Tate Vincent know that she was on the up-and-up. She planned to get her son back the legal way. Justice would side with the biological mother.

Sylvia had to believe that, even though, as an investigative reporter, she'd seen too many cases fouled up in court with corrupt judges and equally corrupt attorneys. She marched ahead of Rosa, C.W. and her son, determined to get the ball rolling as soon as she could get a call through to a lawyer she knew in San Antonio. The same one she'd used when she'd filed for divorce from Miguel Tikas a year and a half ago, before she'd known she was pregnant.

With her resolve strengthened, she followed the smell of food toward the kitchen, ever aware of the people at her back.

She passed an open doorway to an office the size of her old apartment. Tate Vincent stood looking out double French doors, his hand pressing a cell phone to his ear. "Tell him I want it done ASAP. The sooner we know something the better off we all are. Tomorrow morning would be best. Have Dr. Richards call to confirm."

Sylvia paused. Now would be a good time to ask Tate if she could use a telephone. Her cell phone had sketchy reception this far out of Austin, the charger lost with the contents of her car.

When Tate Vincent turned toward her, his brows snapped together in a frown. "What are you doing here?"

His abrupt demand raised the hairs on the back of her neck. Before she could answer, Rosa stepped up beside her.

"She's on her way to the dining room." The Hispanic woman jerked her head, indicating Sylvia should keep walking.

C.W. ducked into the office, Jacob perched on his shoulder. "Someone wants to see you."

Even before C.W. got close, Jacob was leaning toward Tate.

Tate held out his hands and plucked Jacob off C.W.'s shoulders. "Come here, Jake."

Rosa hooked Sylvia's arm with an iron grip. "Come with me."

Sylvia's gaze remained on Tate and Jacob until Rosa jerked her past the office with a violent tug.

"Okay, okay, you don't have to get mean. I'm coming." If she could afford to be nasty, Sylvia would have jerked back as hard as she could, hopefully dropping Rosa on her cranky butt. But she couldn't. If she wanted custody of her son, she had to make nice to the people who held Jacob. One in particular who had enough money to buy a judge of his own.

Deep down, Sylvia realized the difficulties she faced going up against a financial giant like Tate Vincent. The man had unlimited funds at his disposal. He could make the court case last for years with custody of Jacob remaining with him throughout.

Her footsteps faltered and she came to a halt before they reached the kitchen. "I'm too dirty. Besides, I'm not hungry."

"Tough. The boss wants you to eat. So you will eat if I have to force feed you." Rosa stepped into a formal dining room, Sylvia's arm still in her grip. She whipped Sylvia around and nearly tripped her into a padded seat at the dinner table.

Broad windows lined one wall overlooking a field dotted with horses, tails swishing in the late-evening sun. A perfect setting for dinner. A perfect home for a child to grow up in. A place Sylvia could never hope to own, not as a single mom, an investigative reporter, no less. What kind of life could she offer her son? Nothing like this. But she would give him all the love she had in her heart. That had to count for something.

As she'd been staring out at the hill country, Maria moved in and out of the room carrying trays laden with food. She'd laid out on the smooth wood surface of the long mahogany dining table an array of platters brimming with tortillas, sizzling fajitas, rice, refried beans and fluffy mounds of green guacamole.

Sylvia loved Mexican food, her mouth watering despite herself. The hole in her stomach overrode the worry eating at her insides. If she planned on fighting for her son, she'd better keep her energy up.

Rosa stood over her, her arms crossed over her chest like the tough street cop. "Eat."

Hunger trumped anger and Sylvia lifted a fork, piling spicy chicken into a light flour tortilla. She ate like a starving person, unsure of where or when her next meal would come. If Tate decided to throw her out, she'd have nothing to live on, no money, no food, no home to go to. Basically, she was at his mercy.

Tate Vincent stood in the living room, holding Jake in his arms. The open floor plan allowed him to monitor Sylvia's movements. The blonde shoveled food onto her plate like there was no tomorrow. And maybe the events of the past six months made her feel that way. If her waist measurement was any indication, she hadn't been eating enough food to keep healthy.

While Maria had shown Sylvia to her room, Tate had called his lawyer, asking him to check into the information Sylvia had given him regarding Jake's birth mother. Or, if Sylvia was to be believed, the woman who'd masqueraded as Jake's birth mother.

Tate had pulled Jake's birth certificate from his file of important papers and studied it. Again, he couldn't tell if it was real or not. Even his attorney hadn't picked up that it was a fake. At this point, Tate didn't know who the faker was, Beth Kirksey or Sylvia Michaels. He'd left a call out to Brandon, a buddy of his on the San Antonio police force, to verify whether or not Beth Kirksey had really died and her cause of death, if she had.

Even if Ms. Kirksey was dead, it proved nothing.

Tate's cell phone vibrated in his pants pocket. Juggling Jake on one arm, he checked the caller ID. His buddy from SAPD. His stomach twisted as he pressed the cell phone to his ear. "Yeah."

"Tate, Brandon Walker here."

"What did you find out?"

"Beth Kirksey died a week ago. She was struck down by a car that jumped the corner she'd been working. The vehicle hit her head-on and left the scene of the accident without rendering assistance."

Tate's arm tightened around Jake until the little guy squirmed. "Any idea who did it?"

"Still looking for the car. A witness reported seeing a black Hummer with chrome grills speeding away from the scene. Not sure it was the one that hit her, but it's our only lead."

"What did you mean 'the corner she was working'?"

"You know. Her corner." Brandon paused and then cleared his throat. "You didn't know? Beth Kirksey goes by the name Bunny. She's one of the local hookers we've hauled in on occasion for prostitution."

The air left Tate's lungs. For a moment or two he didn't say anything. When the silence stretched on, he swallowed past the lump building in his throat. "Uh, thanks, Brandon."

"Anything else I can do for you, just let me know."

"I might be taking you up on that," Tate said quietly. He clicked the off button and slid the phone into his pocket. Then he hugged Jake so hard, the boy squealed and patted Tate's face.

"Sorry, little man." His eyes burned, but Tate refused to surrender. Not yet. Just because Beth Kirksey was dead didn't mean she wasn't Jake's mother. Tomorrow his family physician was making a house call to collect the DNA samples. Until then, Tate refused to give up hope. Jake was his, damn it!

He carried his little boy into the dining room, intent on telling the trespasser just that.

Rosa stood at Sylvia's shoulder, her arms crossed over her chest.

Tate almost laughed at her stance, sure she'd used the intimidating glare on more than one traffic violator in her job as an Austin cop.

He was surprised Sylvia could eat while Rosa stood over her. But she finished off one fajita and loaded another tortilla with chicken. She must be really hungry.

A twinge of guilt threatened to creep into Tate, which he promptly squashed. After all, this woman threatened the only family he had left. Jake reached out and grabbed Tate's ear and giggled.

Sylvia had raised the tortilla to her mouth to take a bite. Her hand froze, her lips open and ready. When Jake giggled again, her face paled and she turned in her chair. Her face softening as soon as her gaze took in Tate and Jake.

"Oh, baby. Look at you all grown-up." She choked on the last word, the fajita falling to the plate, forgotten. She wiped her fingers on her napkin and stood next to her chair.

"Don't try anything, lady," Rosa said, taking a step closer, putting her body between Tate and Sylvia.

"It's okay, Rosa," Tate said.

"I'll tell you when it's okay. I'm Jake's bodyguard," she said. "If I think he needs protecting, I'll do it."

Tate chuckled. "Always the protector, aren't you?"

"Damn right. And I can take you, too, if I have to." Without turning her back on Sylvia, Rosa asked over her shoulder, "Want me to take Jake to the kitchen?"

Tate stared at Sylvia, whose eyes swam with unshed tears. "Promise to keep your hands to yourself?"

She dragged in a deep, shaky breath and let it out before she nodded. "I do."

"Then I take it you wouldn't mind if Jake and I join you at the dinner table?"

Sylvia's mouth twisted into a sorry attempt at a smile. "It's your table. I'm the one who doesn't belong."

Tate's jaw tightened, but he refused to rise to her words. "Right." He glanced down at his son. "Jake, do you think you can control your urge to throw your food just this once?"

Jake patted his sticky palm against Tate's face. "Da, da, da."

"I'll take that as a yes." Tate tilted his head toward Jake's bodyguard. "Rosa, could you bring Jake's chair?"

She stared at Sylvia and back at Tate before she responded. *"Sí, Señor."*

"Rosa. Stop with the *señor,* already." Tate shook his head. "I pulled your ponytails, we should be able to call each other by our first names for heaven's sake."

"I work for you now. How will you ever trust me to do my job if I'm all casual?"

"Do you love Jake?"

Rosa's back straightened and she stood as tall as her five-feet-three-inch frame could hold her. "Yes, I do."

"Then I trust you to do the best you can to protect him. Now, would you please get that chair?"

"Yes, sir—" She shrugged, a faint flush creeping into

dark-skinned cheeks. "Tate. Yes, Tate." She glared at Sylvia. "Don't do anything dumb."

Sylvia held up both hands in surrender. "I won't."

After Rosa left the room, Tate hooked a chair with his foot and pulled it out at the end of the table beside where Sylvia sat.

"Thanks for trusting me enough to let me stay under the same roof as my son."

"Who said I trusted you?"

"Well, I thought..." Sylvia remained standing, her hands twisting together, her gaze never leaving Jake.

Tate remembered a soldier in the Afghan desert who'd been lost for days without water who had a similar look when handed a canteen of water. That desperately needy look of someone starved for something.

"Do you want to hold him?" He knew the answer before the words left his mouth.

Sylvia nodded once. "More than I want to breathe."

"Sit down and I'll consider it."

As she maneuvered the chair away from the table, a loud pop pierced the silence and glass splintered across the room from a bullet-size hole in the large plate glass windows.

"Get down!" Tate yelled, dropping to the ground, Jake clutched to his chest.

Sylvia stood frozen, her hands still clinging to the back of the chair.

Another pop, splintered the wood on the back of the chair.

Tate reached out and knocked the backs of her knees with his free arm.

Her legs buckled and Sylvia dropped to the ground as another round completely shattered the window, sending shards of glass onto the wood flooring.

Chapter Six

Sylvia lay on the floor, her breath coming in shallow pants, afraid to move should another barrage of bullets come slicing through the air.

Tate shielded Jake with his body, as he inched toward where Sylvia lay on the floor. "Are you okay?"

Sylvia nodded, words lodged behind a giant lump of fear in her throat.

"Who the hell would be shooting at us?" Keeping Jacob low, Tate lifted his head above the table.

"Stay down!" C.W. ran past the dining room, a rifle clutched in each hand. Rosa appeared in the entrance to the dining room, holding a high chair. "What the hell?" She dropped the high chair against the smooth Mexican tile of the hallway and grabbed the rifle C.W. threw her way.

"Tate," Rosa squatted, pointing a finger at Tate as he tried to rise high enough to see through the window. "Do as C.W. said. You have to protect Jake."

Tate hesitated, then he dropped below the table, his mouth a straight, thin line, his grip on Jacob tightening. "I've got it covered here. You two find the bastard."

C.W. raced away, but Rosa stood out of range of the open window. "You sure you don't need me here,

Tate?" She nodded her head toward Sylvia. "Could be a setup."

Tate stared across the floor at Sylvia.

She kept her gaze level. "Why would I have someone shoot at me?"

Rosa snorted. "Could be he was a lousy shot. Maybe the shooter was aiming for Tate."

Sylvia shook her head, staring straight at Tate. "I wouldn't put Jacob in danger. You have to believe me."

"Go on, Rosa," Tate said, his gaze still on Sylvia. "And be careful."

Rosa frowned. "Same to ya, boss." She turned, weapon in hand, and ran down the hallway as fast as she could, one leg stiff, emphasizing her limp.

"What the hell's going on?" Tate asked, setting Jacob on the floor in front of him, keeping his profile and Jacob's as low to the floor as possible.

Guilt ate at Sylvia as she watched Jacob pull himself up on the legs of the chair next to him. "I shouldn't have come."

"I wish the hell you hadn't, but now that you're here, is there more to this story you haven't told me?"

Sylvia plucked at the splinters of wood from the chair, pulling them from the Persian rug beneath the table to keep Jacob from getting his hands on them. "When I was searching and questioning people in Mexico about Jake's disappearance, someone shot at me. I thought it was a random drive-by, drug war shooting. Then when I moved my search to San Antonio, I kept getting that feeling that someone was following me."

She looked up at Tate. "If I'd known they would put Jacob in danger, I…" A look at Jacob, using the chair legs to pull himself up to a standing position, made her throat ache. "Believe me, I don't want any harm to come to my son."

The child stared across at her, a smile lighting his face. He reached out with a chubby fist. "Da, da, da."

"I don't know what to believe anymore." Tate kept a hand looped around Jacob's belly, steadying the wobbly baby.

Jacob leaned against the hand, reaching out to Sylvia in an attempt to move in her direction. A frown drew his light blond brows together, his baby-blue eyes growing stormy.

Laughter bubbled up in Sylvia's chest, despite the danger, despite the fight she'd have on her hands proving that this was her son. For deep in her heart, she knew. "He always did have a fierce frown. Even as an infant." She rose to a crouch and inched toward her baby. "You don't know how hard I prayed for this day. Hi, little man." She reached out, her gaze alternating between Jacob and Tate, afraid that the multimillionaire would stop her from touching the baby.

Careful to keep her head below the tabletop and from view of the shattered window, she moved closer and sat cross-legged on the floor in front of Jacob, wincing at the sharp stab of pain in her injured leg.

Tate's jaw tightened, but he didn't draw the baby back. Instead, he loosened his hold around Jacob's belly and let the boy sway in Sylvia's direction.

The little guy giggled and took a step holding on to the leg of the chair with one hand, his other hand reaching toward her.

A swell of joy filled Sylvia's chest as Jacob let go of the chair leg and fell into her arms.

The scent of baby shampoo wafted beneath her nose,

the fine blond hairs tickling her chin as he pressed his hands against her chest.

Tate regretted letting Sylvia hold Jake as soon as the baby landed in her arms. The resemblance was so strong, it hit Tate like a punch to the gut. Both had light golden, straight blond hair, both had the baby-blue eyes and pale skin. The tilt of Jake's nose was the exact duplicate of his mother's—

Tate fisted his hands. The DNA testing had not yet been done. Until then, his claim to Jake was legal and binding. The family physician would be out the following morning to draw blood samples from both Jake and this stranger who *claimed* to be his mother. In the meantime, he'd keep a close eye on the interloper and an even closer eye on his son.

Sylvia stared down at the baby looking up at her, her eyes suspiciously bright. "Oh, Jacob, you're such a big boy." She looked up at Tate with wonder shining in her eyes. "You call him Jake."

Tate nodded, his teeth grinding against each other. The way the woman held his son looked natural, touching, too sweet. "I named him after my father."

"I named him after my father, too." She brushed her cheek against Jake's, closing her eyes and inhaling. "He smells like baby shampoo and green beans." Her eyes opened and she smiled across the baby. "He was just starting to eat rice cereal when he was—" She gulped, a tear slipping from the corner of her eye.

Tate scooted closer, keeping his profile low. Without thinking, his hand came up and, with the pad of his thumb, he brushed the tear from her cheek.

"I'd almost given up hope," she whispered, leaning into his open palm.

As soon as her cheek touched his hand, an electric jolt rammed through his body. Tate jerked his arm back.

Sylvia's eyes widened and she stared into his gaze. "I'm sorry. I didn't mean to…" Her gaze sank to the baby in front of her. "It's just that I've been searching so long." Her voice dropped to a whisper. "Alone."

If he hadn't been as close as he was, he'd never have heard the last word. "Sylvia, where's your child's father? Why isn't he helping?"

Sylvia's lips twisted. "I don't think he ever wanted Jacob. We separated when I was only a month pregnant. Miguel just wanted to make my life difficult. He took more pleasure in blaming me for everything that went wrong—Jacob's disappearance…our divorce."

"Bastard." Tate couldn't imagine a father giving up on his own child. Not on Jake. The hardness in his chest softened as he touched Jake's blond hair, the strands softer than silk.

A sigh escaped Sylvia's lips. "He did help me with the Mexican authorities. But crime is out of control in Mexico. More and more kidnappings are being reported, inundating the system. I spent an entire week wading through red tape with the American Embassy and the Mexican police. They did nothing. And the longer they took, I just knew, Jacob would be taken farther and farther away."

The thought of his son being taken away to God knew where made Tate's chest hurt. His hand pressed against his sternum as he asked, "How'd you trace Jake here all the way from Mexico?"

"I advertised a reward for my son's return." She caressed Jacob's cheek. "I went through at least a thousand leads before a man slipped into my hotel room one night and practically scared me to death. He told me about a human trafficking ring stealing babies in Mexico and sending them to San Antonio, Texas, where they were put up for adoption…to the highest bidder." Her brows narrowed, her tone hardening. "They were auctioning babies."

An image of Sylvia alone in her hotel room with a dangerous stranger appeared in Tate's mind and he didn't like it. Her delicate features didn't hide her tenacious spirit, but how would she have resisted if a man wanted to harm her? "Did he threaten you?"

"No. Actually, he looked more scared than I felt."

"You trusted this man's word?"

"I couldn't discount any information. I had to follow it whether or not it was a dead end. When someone shot at me on the street right after I'd met with the informant, my gut told me this was one lead I needed to follow up on."

"What about the other leads?"

"All of them were desperate attempts to claim the reward. Nothing substantial." The hollow look in her eyes told the story.

If Tate were in the same situation every dead end would rip another piece from his heart, he could imagine how it had been for Sylvia. He fought to remain neutral, to not get sucked into her tale. After all, she could be lying to him, hoping to collect on any sign of weakness. "How did you know this guy was telling the truth?"

"I'm a freelance reporter. I did a piece on gangs in San Antonio two years ago. I got in touch with some of my contacts and had them do some asking around." Her face paled. "They said the prostitutes had mentioned something about babies being sold. I had to follow the lead."

"That's when you found out about Beth Kirksey?"

"I flew to San Antonio and questioned several of the ladies. Eventually I heard about a hooker named Bunny, aka Beth Kirksey. Apparently she had a baby and put it up for adoption as soon as it was born."

A pinch of relief filled Tate. "There you go. I adopted that baby. Beth Kirksey was Jake's mother."

"Except Beth's baby was adopted at birth two weeks before you adopted Jake. I tracked down the adoptive parents. She sold that one for twenty thousand dollars." Sylvia's lips thinned. "My baby was four months old. That was six months ago." She stared down at Jacob. "How old is Jake?"

Tate hesitated. Then he heaved a sigh. "Ten months yesterday."

Sylvia's gaze returned to claim Tate's.

He was saved from further conjecture by the arrival of Rosa. "C.W. hopped on a horse. Whoever shot at you is probably long gone. I heard the sound of an engine as we hit the door on the way out." As if seeing Sylvia for the first time, Rosa glared. "What's she doing with Jake?"

Tate stood, lifting Jake up into his arms, away from Sylvia. "Call the sheriff about the shooting. I want whoever did it caught."

"Will do." Rosa glanced from Tate to Sylvia and back. "You sure she didn't set you up?"

"No, I'm not certain. But we'll have to take her at face value for now."

"I don't like it, Señor Vincent," Rosa said.

"Tate," he insisted.

"Tate." Rosa's glare could have burned a hole in Sylvia.

Tate almost laughed out loud, but the gravity of what

had just happened sobered him. "Go on, Rosa. Make that call."

She left the room, throwing barbed glances back at Sylvia, daring the interloper to make a move. Any move. Rosa would take her down, bum leg or not.

Tate looked over the top of Jake's pale blond head, his lips pressing together. He couldn't afford to get soft-hearted with Sylvia Michaels. Jake represented his world. The only family he had left. He refused to give up on the boy.

He extended a hand to Sylvia. "I'm not saying I buy any of what you just told me. I sent for my family doctor. He'll be here tomorrow to draw blood or swab cheeks, whatever he has to do to collect DNA samples."

He expected her to look scared, maybe uncertain about his announcement. Instead of looking shaken at his declaration, she smiled at the boy in Tate's arms. "Good. The sooner we have proof, the sooner I get my son back."

His arm tightened around Jake. "Don't count on it. Jake's mine until the courts convince me otherwise. In the meantime, I'm keeping an eye on you." He nodded toward the shattered window. "You might be a fake, but those bullets weren't. If anything happens to my son and I find out you had something to do with it, well, let's just say we have ways of dealing justice here in Texas."

Chapter Seven

Boots clattered up the wooden porch, breaking the strained silence stretching between Sylvia and Tate.

"Tate? You two okay?" C.W. burst into the room, his deeply tanned skin red and shining with sweat.

"Yeah, C.W. We're good." Tate hefted Jake to his other arm. "What did you find?"

Sylvia's glance darted to the shattered window. Nothing moved in the field beyond the house. But then, she hadn't seen anything move before the shooting began.

C.W. dragged his cowboy hat off his head and slapped it against his jeans, dust flying off in a powdery cloud. "I grabbed Frisco and followed the tracks of a four-wheeler to the edge of your property along the highway. He had the jump on me by a few minutes. I never caught him."

"Did you get a look at the shooter?" Tate asked.

C.W. shook his head. "No. All I had was the tracks to go on. They led up to a break in the fence close to the highway. Someone cut the barbed wire. Anyway, the ATV had disappeared. There were truck-tire marks in the dust and rubber skid marks on the pavement. Whoever lit out of here, didn't mind losing a layer of treads."

"Damn—" The millionaire caught himself short of cursing with Jake in his arms.

"Hey! No swearing around Jake." Rosa reappeared

around a corner. "I called the sheriff. He'll be back here in under fifteen." She reached for Jacob. "Let me take the little guy to his room."

Tate's brows furrowed, but he let his nanny/bodyguard take charge of the boy. "Move Jake's crib to a room without windows. I don't want anyone taking potshots at the house and hitting him."

"I'll set up his bed in your closet."

Sylvia frowned. "A closet? Isn't that extreme, locking a child in the closet?"

Rosa chuckled. "Some people have smaller bedrooms than Mr. Vincent's closet."

"Tate." The man shook his head. "Stop calling me Mr. Vincent. You're making me feel old. However, putting Jake in my closet is an excellent idea, Rosie."

Rosa frowned. "It's Rosa to you, Mr. Vincent." She gathered the boy in her arms and headed toward the nursery.

C.W. busted out laughing, immediately sobering. "Sorry, Tate. She's a handful, that one."

Tate shook his head. "Sometimes I wonder why I hired her."

"Because she knows this place as well as you do." C.W. nodded in the direction Rosa went with Jake. "And she's the best person for the job of protecting Jake."

"Darn right, I am." Rosa's voice carried down the hallway.

Tate turned to C.W. "Let me know when the sheriff arrives."

"Will do. I'll get the boys on the job repairing the cut fence."

"Thanks." Tate walked away, stopped and turned back. "Tell them to carry some protection."

C.W. saluted Tate with the tips of two fingers. "Roger that."

Tate disappeared into his office, closing the door behind him.

"Well, hell's bells." Sylvia threw her hands into the air. "You'd think getting shot at was an everyday occurrence with the infamous Mr. Tate Vincent."

C.W. twirled his hat in his hand, his lips twisting into a wry grin. "Used to be in Afghanistan."

"Weren't you and Vincent on active duty together during Operation Enduring Freedom?"

C.W.'s smile faded. "Yeah, so what?"

"Has he always been this cryptic?"

The smile returned. "No, he was much worse. That's Vincent for you. Now, if you don't mind, I've got work to do."

"Don't let me hold you up." She turned around, not exactly sure what to do with herself. "I'm just surprised the great Tate Vincent doesn't have a guard posted on me at all times."

"Guess he figures you're not much of a threat to him."

She snorted. "Nice to know."

"Says a lot. Considering his father was stabbed by a trespasser. He later died of complications from the wounds."

Sylvia's heart clenched in her chest. "I'd read something about that."

"Almost turned into a bum rap for Tate."

Sylvia nodded, recalling the front pages of the San Antonio newspaper blaming Tate for the stabbing. "The person closest is often the first person suspected in domestic violence," she whispered softly. Unscrupulous reporters sensationalized the story, making the public believe Tate had either stabbed his own father or paid someone to do it for him.

"Media tried to crucify him saying that he wanted his hands on the land sooner, so he paid someone to kill his father," C.W. said. He looked over his shoulder. "Not that Tate would want me to be telling tales, but I thought you should know why he's so suspicious."

It had only been eight months ago. Right before Sylvia's trip to Mexico. The police report, the news headlines. Not until she'd returned to San Antonio did she learn of the final outcome. And only then when she'd been searching for information about the man who'd potentially adopted her son.

The newspapers and television had a field day with the dark and brooding Tate Vincent, convicting him before he had a chance to defend himself. And he hadn't defended himself. The man who'd stabbed his father had been caught, but no one could link him to the only surviving Vincent. "His father's death had nothing to do with me or my son."

"Maybe so or maybe not." C.W. settled his hat on his head. He stared around at the shambles of a dining room. "Maria will have grub in the kitchen."

Despite the fact she'd only downed one fajita, Sylvia wasn't hungry anymore. She'd been shot at. Worse, Jake had been close enough to be hit. Claiming her son may have had more lethal consequences than letting him live his life in the lap of Vincent luxury.

TATE STEPPED OUT ON the deck, the warm night air a welcome respite from the cool air-conditioning of his office. He'd checked on Jake, settled comfortably in his crib in the large walk-in closet adjacent to the master suite. Rosa would sleep in the connecting room. The woman claiming to be Jake's mother had the bedroom at the end of the hallway, far enough away Tate felt confident she wouldn't be a threat to Jake.

Wrapped in the heat of the night, Tate kept to the shadows beneath the rafters. The relative silence of the hill country enveloped him. Crickets chirped, frogs croaked and cicadas hummed raucously.

Tate's lips twitched. That was hill country silence, laced with nature's song. When he stayed in Austin or Houston, he missed the white noise of the countryside, the blare of sirens and horns nothing to compare with the gentle background sounds of the open range.

A board creaked.

Tate stiffened and then relaxed as a waft of cigarette smoke drifted his way.

He leaned against the limestone wall. "I thought you were going home."

Kacee pushed away from the rough-hewn cedar post, her high heels clicking against the dry planks of the deck. She still wore the business suit she'd had on earlier. "I did."

Tate shook his head. "When did you get back?"

"While you were in the shower. I heard you'd been shot at. Sounds like your little trespasser brought trouble with her."

Tate stared out at the night sky, stars twinkling brightly, as if not a care in the universe. How long had it been since he'd hung like a star in the heavens, no worries, no cares? He shrugged. Not since he was a teen. "At least no one was hurt. Any news from Dr. Richards?"

"He called to confirm that he'd be here first thing in the morning."

"What about Double Diamond Ranch? Are they going to sell?"

She took another drag from her cigarette and tossed the glowing remainder over the rail.

Tate made a mental note of where it landed. As dry as it had been, a smoldering cigarette butt could cause the loss of thousands of acres of grasslands. He'd warned Kacee at least a hundred times. What would it take to get it through her hard head?

"Do we always have to talk business?" Kacee leaned close to him, blowing out the fragrant menthol smoke laced with another cloying aroma. Wine. Probably merlot. Kacee liked to drink a glass every night. Helped her to unwind.

She probably needed at least half a bottle as tightly as she was strung. For a woman who could handle the toughest boardroom discussions and keep cool under all the pressure, she did have her crutches. Merlot and the occasional cigarette, habits she'd had long before he'd hired her. Habits no amount of cajoling convinced her to quit.

Her arm hooked through his and she reached up and brushed away the lock of hair hanging down over his forehead. "Look at the moon. Do you ever get tired of looking at the moon? Even in the dirtiest, stinkiest places, the mood shines pure and true. You can always count on it. It'll never let you down."

"Yeah. That's true enough. What brought that on? It's not like you to wax poetic on me."

She shrugged. "Let's just say I'm tired of beating around the bush."

"How so? You never hold your punches, Kacee. If you have something to say, say it."

Leaning into him, she rubbed her cheek against his sleeve. "Sometimes you can't see the nose at the end of your face, Tate Vincent."

Uncomfortable with how close she was, he extricated his arm out of her hold and led her to the swing, hung from the rafters at the end of the porch. "Just how much wine have you had to drink, Kacee? You might want to sit before you fall."

She wiggled free of his hands and walked to the rail, ever composed as the business executive she was. "I haven't been overindulging, if that's what you mean." Kacee spun, swaying slightly. "And I can see more clearly than I've ever seen in the past." Her eyes narrowed, their gray depths darker than the shadows beneath the eaves. "Haven't I always been there for you?"

Tate's brows rose. "Of course. That's why I pay you the big bucks."

She stomped her foot, her brow wrinkling into a fierce frown. "No, I mean when you wanted to buy all those stocks, didn't I get the scoop on that company in Detroit? Wasn't I there to help you make an informed decision?"

"Yes." Too tired to play games, Tate bit down on his tongue. It wasn't like Kacee to talk aimlessly. Something must be bothering her a lot to make her lose focus, more than the wine.

"Wasn't I there when your father took ill? Didn't I help you find an adoption agency that ultimately brought Jake into your life before your father's passing?"

"You did all that."

"I'm good for you, Tate Vincent. We make a great team."

"Agreed. You're the best executive assistant a person could have."

"That's it?" She threw her hands in the air. "After all I've sacrificed for you. That's it?"

"I appreciate all you've done for me. Didn't I give you

a whopping bonus at the end of the year? Didn't I pay for your new car?" Beyond patient, Tate couldn't keep from speaking out. "What's your point, Kacee?"

"God, you're clueless." She stared at him for a long, agonizing moment, then turned her back to him, hugging her arms around her middle. "There is no point."

Tate hesitated before he awkwardly touched her shoulder. "I'm sorry, Kacee. If you thought there was more between us than boss and employee, there is. But it only goes as far as friendship."

She shrugged off his hand. "Thanks. I've got enough friends." Her back stiffened, drawing her up to her full five foot nine inches. "Is there anything I can get you before you turn in? A stock quote, business analysis, staple remover? *Sir?*"

Refusing to rise to Kacee's sarcasm, Tate took the high ground with a level tone. "No, I'm good for the night. Be careful on your drive back into town."

"I'd planned on staying here tonight."

Tate shook his head even before she'd finished her sentence. "You should stay in town. With people taking potshots at the house, I'd rather those who have alternate housing take advantage of it."

"But—"

"Just do it." Patience worn thin, Tate's words came out abrupt, brooking no argument.

"Okay, okay, you don't have to bite my head off."

"Sorry."

"Don't worry about it. I'm used to it." She walked down to the bottom step of the porch before she turned and looked back up at him. "Don't let her get under your skin, Tate. She's bad news."

"What are you talking about?"

"Sylvia Michaels. She's trouble, I tell you. Don't trust

her. Most likely she's lying through her teeth to get something out of the Vincent fortune."

"Don't worry about me. I can take care of myself."

"I know you can. But sometimes you need a little reminder. At times you can be downright gullible."

"That's why I have you." Kacee had street smarts, raised by a single mother on the wrong side of the tracks. She'd been tough, savvy and determined to pull herself out of the slums. That's why Tate had hired her. He'd recognized her tenaciousness and knew she'd serve well, advancing his plans for Vincent Enterprises. But sometimes her past flared up when she pushed the envelope of ethics. "Go home, Kacee."

She pinned Tate with a gaze that lasted uncomfortably long. He refused to look away, refused to give her even a shred of encouragement. They were boss and employee, nothing more. At least on his end of the relationship.

Finally, she looked away and headed off across the yard to her Lexus.

Tate stepped off the porch and went in search of the discarded cigarette butt, Kacee's words rolling over and over in his mind. Why would his executive assistant think he'd let a stray get under his skin? He'd warded off more women than a man had a right to consider. Being one of the most eligible bachelors in the state of Texas didn't help. Women of all shapes, ages and sizes threw themselves in his path in hopes of a fairy-tale happily ever after with the rich playboy.

Why should Sylvia Michaels present any kind of a threat to him? The woman had come to take Jake away from him. That was enough reason for him to hate her and he'd fight her with his last breath to keep his son. Any woman threatening to take Jake away was trouble, as far as he was concerned.

everything she said she was—a mother whose child had been stolen from her. A mother who'd tracked that child over thousands of miles to find him. If the DNA results came back and proved her claim, how could Tate stand in the way of her waltzing out the door with the only family he had left? About to stand and make his presence known, he shifted.

"Look, Tony, I need to know if you've found out any more about the man Beth Kirksey got Jacob from." She listened for a moment. "Nothing? I want to know as soon as you hear anything. And Tony, I need another favor. Can you check on a Kacee LeBlanc, C. W. Middleton and Rosa Garcia? I don't know how long my phone will last. I've lost my charger. I'll contact you in twenty-four hours. I need to know what I'm up against when I try to get my son out of here. No, I won't do anything stupid. But I *will* take my son home," she said, her voice hard-edged.

After she slid the phone closed, she stared out at the stars again, letting her head fall back, her long silky tresses flowing down her back to her smooth, rounded bottom.

Feeling depressingly like a Peeping Tom, Tate realized his window of opportunity to make his presence known had come and gone. He'd have to wait her out or look the fool.

The cell phone in his pocket vibrated, making him jump, shaking the bushes.

Sylvia swung around, her hands jerking into a fighting position, her heart banging against her chest. "Who's there?"

Beside her, leaves rattled and Tate Vincent rose from among the hedges. "Me."

Her pulse skipped a few beats and continued ham-

"If you want to know anything about the people in my employ..." Tate stepped from bushes and out into the open. "All you had to do was ask."

Sylvia crossed her arms over her chest. "I like to do my own checking."

"That's right, you're a freelance reporter."

She straightened, her chin coming up. "That's right. I have my own contacts." She squared off with him, her shoulders thrown back, her chin held high. "I want my son back and I'll do whatever it takes to get him."

Tate closed the distance between them so fast, Sylvia didn't have time to react. "I repeat, until the courts say otherwise, Jake's my son."

The man was too close, casting her into the shadows, blocking the moon and stars with the breadth of his shoulders.

Staring up into his smoldering gaze, with the light from a window glinting off his irises, Sylvia found herself at a loss for words, something she never was. Her pulse throbbed against her temples and her throat dried to the consistency of the parched Texas dust beneath her feet.

"Do you understand?" His voice, low and menacing, had a strange effect on her nerve endings. "Anything happens to my son and I'm holding you personally responsible."

Sylvia gulped to wet the lining of her throat. "He's my son. And I could say the same."

He stared down at her, making her all too aware of the way his chest rose and fell beneath the polo shirt he now wore. The fresh scent of aftershave filled her nostrils, reminding her of her complete lack of sex since she'd divorced Miguel. Only Miguel didn't hold a candle to Tate Vincent. At least four inches taller, Tate's shoulders were broad and muscular, probably from working his ranch like the tabloids liked to report.

Miguel's muscles weren't nearly as defined, nor were they produced from real work. He had his own trainer and weight equipment in his hacienda in Monterrey. But he'd never done a hard day's work like Tate Vincent.

As much as Sylvia hated to admit it, she admired a rich man who wasn't so distanced from his roots that he paid others to do all the dirty work. He'd set a good example for his children. Too bad Jacob wouldn't be one of them.

The last thought made her eyes widen. Never in a million years would she expect Tate Vincent to be the father her son would know growing up. But the image stuck of Tate teaching Jacob to ride a horse…Tate teaching Jacob to mend a fence or work with his hands…Tate teaching Jake about all the animals and the people who made a ranch viable.

The endless possibilities of life on the Vincent ranch, growing up surrounded by everything money could buy and a man who could teach him things Sylvia couldn't was a childhood dream. She'd never ridden a horse or mended a fence. She couldn't even throw a football. Who would be there to teach Jacob how to be a man?

She inched away from Tate, backing away from her feelings of inadequacy. Jacob was her son. She wouldn't abandon him now that she'd found him. She loved him more than life itself. "I'd better go to bed. Tomorrow promises to be an interesting day. You said the doctor would be out to collect DNA samples?" Now she was babbling, but she couldn't help herself. The man flustered her.

The hard line of his jaw softened. "Yes, you should go to bed." His eyes lost their hardness and his lips tipped upward in the corner. He followed her, matching her retreat, step for step. "Did anyone ever tell you that you have very expressive eyes?"

Too late, he'd moved and the moon shone down into her eyes, probably revealing all of her thoughts. "It's a curse."

"Not really. What were you just thinking?"

Close enough she could feel the warmth of his breath on her skin, he made her body hum to life. "N-nothing."

He reached out, cupping her chin. "Nothing?"

"That's right." Her voice squeaked as she tried to maintain a grip on her senses, all of which were whipped into a frenzy, overpowered by a man known for his charm by women all over the world. Sylvia kept telling herself that he was playing with her. Nothing he said or did meant anything to him other than an angle to get what he wanted. That's what rich men did. They used the little people for their own gain. Like Miguel had used her then left her for another woman.

"Then why did you look so sad?" His thumb brushed against her cheek. "If you really think Jake's your son, you should be ecstatic."

"I am." Her heart banged against her chest, her vision dimmed, until all of her focus centered on his mouth. "Very excited."

"What is it about you? I don't trust you any farther than I could throw you." He murmured the words, the content of which should have infuriated her.

Instead she fell under his spell, unable to pull free, unable to think a rational thought. "Is this how you made your millions?" she asked, her voice no more than a whisper.

"How's that?" He leaned close brushing his cheek

against her temple. His fingers circled behind her neck, his thumb stroking the tender skin beneath her ear. "You smell good. What's that scent?"

"Soap." Her head tipped backward of its own accord. "Did you make your millions by charming snakes out of a basket or women into your bed? Because you could, you know."

"Is that what you think?" His mouth brushed her temple, dragging along her cheekbone to hover above her trembling lips. "Tell me, is it working?"

All thoughts ceased. Sylvia could barely process the signals coming in from all of her senses. The man was a flame, she the moth drawn inexorably closer to her demise. And the sad thing was that she could do nothing to stop herself. She swayed closer, her lips sweeping across his in a featherlight brush with temptation.

Somewhere something buzzed. A vibration other than her own pulse slammed against her veins, penetrating her clothing against her hip.

"Damn." Tate stepped away from Sylvia and dug into his pocket, unearthing a cell phone. He stared at the device, reading the caller ID. He flipped the phone open. "What do you want, Kacee?" He hesitated. "I'm sorry, Helen, I thought you might be Kacee. What can I do for you?"

SYLVIA TOOK ANOTHER step back, then another, sucking in a long, much-needed breath to clear her head of the Tate-induced fog. What else could she call it. The man could turn her on. He'd proven that in under thirty seconds. Good Lord. Was she that desperate?

She pressed a hand to her breast and sucked in another breath, the second having no more effect on slowing her pulse or steadying her erratic breathing.

What kind of game was he playing? Was he trying to prove something? That she was an unfit mother? If she wanted the courts to take her seriously, she'd have to prove she was fit. If she wanted to get her son back, she'd have to keep Tate Vincent at a distance.

"Good Lord." With the cell phone pressed to his ear, Tate paced a few steps away and pushed his hand through his dark hair, standing it on end. "Is he going to be all right? Don't even worry about it. I'll manage without him. Tell him to concentrate on getting better." He listened for a minute. "I'll take care of it myself. If you need anything, don't hesitate to call. Thanks for letting me know." He flipped the phone shut and turned toward her. "I don't know what game you're playing, but don't think you're going to get away with it."

Having just had similar thoughts about his game, Sylvia's back straightened. "What are you talking about?"

"You know perfectly well what I'm talking about." In a flash, he grabbed her arms, his fingers digging into the flesh. "I don't take kindly to people who hurt my friends and family."

"I've done nothing to hurt you or your friends."

"Then how do you explain the shots fired earlier?" he demanded, shaking her.

"They were shooting at me, too!" She pulled at his fingertips, trying to dislodge his iron grip. The fury in his face frightening her more than the pain where his fingers clamped into her arms.

"Are you sure they weren't shooting at me? Were they aiming to kill me or just as a warning to pay whatever price you demand?"

"I don't know. Why don't you ask the shooter?" she shouted back at him.

"You said you'd do what it takes to get your son back. Does that include murder?"

Sylvia gasped. For a long moment, she stared up into Tate's glaring eyes before she answered honestly. "I don't know. All I do know is that I'd do anything necessary to protect my son. I sure as heck wouldn't hire someone to shoot at the man holding him."

Tate shoved her away. "My close friend, Dr. Allen Richards, the man who was supposed to collect DNA samples, was run off the road by someone less than an hour ago."

Sylvia stood stock-still, the blood leaving her head, making her dizzy. She forced herself to think. "Will he be all right?"

"Yes, but he won't be here tomorrow as planned."

She let go of the breath she hadn't realized she'd been holding and sagged against his grip. "Thank God."

"That he won't be here?"

"No, that he lived to tell you about it."

Tate released one arm and pressed a finger to her chest. "If I find out that you had anything to do with this, I'll…"

"You'll what?" She refused to show her fear, standing as straight as she could, glaring up at him with all the attitude she could muster while being manhandled. "As far as I know, you could be in on the whole setup, stealing babies and selling them to the highest bidder. How do I know you aren't the kingpin to the entire operation?"

"Watch what you say, woman."

"Why? What will you do, Tate Vincent? What will you do that could be worse than stealing my baby?" She jerked her arm free from his grip and stepped back. "You could have set up the shooting, aiming for me. Get rid of the mother and you're free to keep Jacob. Was that the plan all along? Are you the one trying to kill me?"

Chapter Eight

Before Tate could respond to her accusation, his cell phone buzzed with an incoming text message.

Sylvia turned and left him standing there, Tate too taken aback to follow.

He pulled his phone from his pocket and, through a haze of rage, read Kacee's message. "911. Call me."

Afraid of more bad news concerning his friend Dr. Richards, Tate let Sylvia get away as he punched the speed dial for Kacee.

"Tate! Thank God. Have you heard from Helen Richards?"

"Yes."

"Can you believe what happened to Allen?"

"Kacee, do you have anything else you want to report that I don't already know?"

The screen door creaked open and slammed shut on the house. Sylvia had gone inside. Although she'd left his sight, everything about where he stood radiated her presence. From the moonlight to the smell of dust in the air. Tate couldn't get her out of his head. Nor could he discount the words she'd flung in his face.

He still didn't know whether she'd been responsible for Dr. Richards's accident. She'd been with him when the accident occurred so he couldn't pin blame directly on her, though he wanted to. It would make it much easier for him to hate her if she was responsible for running his friend off the road and for the shooting earlier. She'd driven him over the edge with her taunts and her blue-eyed gaze and her pale skin, so delicate and clear, the glow of her blond hair in the moonlight.

Damn her! Tate punched his fist into the solid cedar post of the porch, the pain jolting him back to his senses. His hand throbbed, his knuckles bruised and bleeding. In retrospect, maybe hitting the post wasn't such a good idea. But it had accomplished one thing. It had helped him to focus on what was important: Jake.

That woman was inside with Jake while Tate stood outside. Whoever had shot at the house could still be around. Whoever had run Dr. Richards off the road could be lying in wait for any one of his staff, including him. If Sylvia Michaels really was determined to get her son back, would she do anything? Even hire a killer? Or would she do the job herself?

"Kacee, I gotta go."

"Tate, I contacted a buddy of mine in private investigations. He's doing a check on your Sylvia Michaels."

"Good. Let me know what he finds."

"I will."

"I'll talk to you tomorrow."

"Tate?"

"What, Kacee?"

"Remember what I said. Trouble with a capital *T*."

His grip tightened on the phone as his lips recalled the feel of Sylvia's against his own. "I already know it."

SYLVIA PAUSED OUTSIDE the door to the room she'd been assigned. What had just happened out there in the bushes? Why had she reacted so strongly to a perfect stranger? She'd almost kissed the man! And the scary thought was that she wanted to do it.

She pressed shaking fingertips to her mouth, the nerve endings in her lips jumping at the touch. He'd smelled of mint and leather, his body generating heat that scorched her senses.

How could she even consider kissing a man who held her life and happiness in his grasp? A man with enough money to buy every judge in the state of Texas.

Tate Vincent was nothing to her. Nothing but the man who'd been duped into adopting her stolen baby. A man she'd have to fight in court to regain custody of her son.

Jacob. Sweet, angelic Jacob.

An ache the size of Texas built in her, filling her chest. She let it push out thoughts of kissing the multimillionaire rancher with the midnight-black hair. She let the ache consume her and remind her what was most important. Getting her son back.

More than anything, she wanted to see Jacob before she called it a night and attempted to sleep. As much as had gone on in the past twenty-four hours, she should be exhausted. Too jumpy and appalled by her recent actions, sleep was the furthest thing from her mind.

Finally, she'd found her baby. The flutter of excitement in her belly wouldn't dissipate. Six months of searching and she'd finally found him. And he was beautiful, healthy and appeared to be happy.

She longed to go to him and hold him, touch his face, count his fingers and toes as she had done when she'd first held him in the delivery room of Santa Rosa Hospital in San Antonio. Her son. The child she'd loved with all her heart was in a room down the hall.

Before she realized it, she'd taken several steps toward the room she suspected was the master suite.

"Do it, *chica*. Give me a reason to cut you down."

Sylvia yelped and dodged sideways, slamming her back against the wall to face the woman who'd sneaked up on her.

A smirk lifted one corner of Rosa's dark lips, her brown-black eyes narrowed into slits. "Take one more step and I'll consider it an attack on Jake. That's all the excuse I need to take you out."

Sylvia recognized a deep-seated rage in the woman and wondered again if she was the right person for the job of caregiver and bodyguard to her son. Dragging in a deep, steadying breath, Sylvia pushed herself off the wall and faced Rosa. "I'm not afraid of you," she lied.

Rosa stepped forward until she stood toe-to-toe with Sylvia. "You should be," she whispered in a low, dangerous tone.

"Let it go, Rosie." Tate Vincent stepped into the hallway, his hands on his hips.

The tough Hispanic woman rolled her eyes without taking her gaze off Sylvia. "It's Rosa, not Rosie, Mr. Vincent."

"Really, Rosie, call me Tate. Now go check on Jake and call it a night."

Her gaze narrowed even more at Sylvia. "You sure?"

Tate pushed a hand through his hair. The fine lines beside his eyes etched deeper. "It's been a long day. Go to bed."

Rosa blew a breath out her nose like a raging bull before she backed away from Sylvia.

Sylvia let her muscles relax a little, unclenching her fists at her sides.

"I still think she bears watching, Mr. Vincent," Rosa said.

He shook his head, a hint of a smile tipping the corner of his lips upward.

The exhaustion in his face and the simple gesture of a half smile made Sylvia's stomach turn flips. After the near kiss outside, she hadn't stopped thinking about Tate Vincent and his darned lips. Now she found herself staring at them again.

She closed her eyes and dragged in a deep breath. "You're right. It's been a long day. If you don't mind, I'll call it a night."

"And no midnight wandering," Rosa warned. "I sleep lightly and so does Mr. Vincent."

"Rosa," Tate growled.

"Okay, okay, keep your shirt on, Tate. I'm going."

Tate Vincent squared off with Sylvia. "It's true. Both of us will be sleeping light and watching out for Jake."

Sylvia crossed her arms over her chest. "You do that. I wouldn't want anything to happen to my son. I will get him back if it's the last thing I do."

Rosa pushed past Sylvia, bumping her intentionally with her shoulder. "Keep it up and it might just be the last thing you *attempt* to do."

When Rosa had cleared the hallway, Tate stayed, staring at Sylvia for a long moment. Finally, he sighed. "Get some rest. Tomorrow you, me and Jake will take a trip into Austin to get that DNA testing done." Then he followed Rosa to the end of the hallway.

Sylvia took a deep breath and let it out. Maybe Rosa was the right one to keep Jake safe. She had the heart of a lioness and could intimidate the heck out of anyone.

So much for seeing her son before she turned in, the decision made for her by Tate and Rosa. She'd have more of a chance facing off with a gang than going up against Rosa again.

Suddenly the day's events weighed in, exhaustion destroying her will to continue the fight. For now. Today she'd found her son. Tomorrow would be another day.

She opened the door and stepped inside, closing it behind her. The room she'd been assigned had a luxurious connecting bathroom lined in granite and tumbled marble. She shed her clothing and climbed into the shower, letting the warm cascade soothe her jangled nerves. The water stung the cut on her leg and she winced. She hoped her tetanus shot was up to date.

After scrubbing the Texas dust from her body and shampooing her hair, Sylvia stepped from the shower and wrapped herself in a warm, fluffy towel. Already anticipating the pillow, she didn't bother looking through the clothing Rosa had delivered earlier. She padded across the cool, hardwood floor to the four-poster bed, pulled the white eyelet coverlet aside and lay down, towel and all. She'd thought she would find it hard to go to sleep, but before she could count ten sheep, her eyes closed, darkness claiming the night.

A NOISE JERKED TATE from a light sleep and he darted out of the bed, headed straight for his closet and Jake.

Rosa stood over the crib in the closet, the door to the connecting room opened wide. "Shh. He's still asleep."

"What was that noise?"

"I don't know. Something outside. Do you want me to check or watch Jake?"

"I'll check. You stay here." He turned to go, pulling a pair of jeans over his boxers, then slipping his bare feet into cowboy boots.

He ran down the hallway and almost plowed into

Sylvia as she emerged from her doorway holding a towel around her naked body and pushing her lush blond hair from her face. "What's going on?"

"I don't know. Stay put and keep out of trouble."

C.W. burst through the back door, shouting, "The barn's on fire! The barn's on fire!" He didn't wait for a response, letting the door slam closed behind him as he ran out into the night.

Tate followed at a dead run, exploding out into the yard to see a wall of flame rising from the roof of the hundred-and-fifty-year-old barn his great-grandfather had built. Horses screamed inside as C.W. flung the double doors open and dove inside.

At least eight horses were stabled in the barn, all screaming, their neighs rising with the crackling flames.

By the time he entered the barn, smoke choked the air, singeing Tate's lungs.

Sassy nearly knocked him over racing for the door, the sorrel mare's eyes crazed, her nostrils flared in the light from the rising flames. C.W. struggled to lead the Vincent prized quarterhorse mare, Fandango, out of her stall. She reared, her hooves flailing in the air, knocking C.W. to the ground.

Tate rushed forward, snatching at the lead rope, leaning all of his weight on it, forcing the horse to stand on all four hooves, bringing the frightened animal under control.

C.W. rolled against the side of the stall and staggered to his feet, coughing. He helped Tate drag the horse out of the stall. Once the beast cleared the barn door, the men released the lead and raced back into smoke.

A shadowy figure stood in front of one of the stalls, struggling to unlatch the heavy clasps. In the swirling smoke, a wisp of blond hair caught Tate's attention. "Sylvia! What the hell?"

She coughed and shoved at the metal catch. The latch released and the heavy wooden door swung out. Even before the door was fully open, the gelding inside slammed into the wood, throwing Sylvia to the ground.

Tate slapped the horse's flanks, sending him in the direction of the barn opening, before he helped Sylvia to her feet. "Get out of here!" he shouted over the roar of the fire.

"No." Her cheeks flushed from the heat and smudged with smoke, Sylvia climbed to her feet and ran for the next stall door. "You can't let the animals die!"

He raced after her, grabbing her shoulder. "You'll die if you stay in here. Go!" He pushed her in the direction of the door, but she refused to go.

"You're wasting time better spent saving your horses." She coughed, bending low to avoid the worst of the smoke.

The horse behind the stall door kicked the wooden walls and screamed in the billowing smoke. Tate read the engraving on the door.

Diablo.

Sylvia reached for the stall door, grasped the iron latch and shoved it hard, opening it in one move. Tate caught the door before it could knock her down, reaching inside for the horse's lead. The stallion reared, jerking the rope through Tate's hand, burning through the calluses on his palms. He held fast, refusing to let the horse die in the fire or trample Sylvia.

He tugged with all his might, edging the horse inch by hard-won inch out of the stall. At last they were free of the walls. Still, Diablo couldn't see in the smoke-choked building. He danced around in a circle before Tate could lead him toward what he hoped was the barn entrance. At last he got the horse out, slapping his rump hard to hurry him along.

C.W. shouted, "One more in the corner stall. I'll get him!"

"No, you and Sylvia get the hell out of here."

"No can do, boss man." C.W. coughed and started back into the barn.

"That's an order. Get out!" Tate ran back into the burning inferno. Where had Sylvia gone? Was she still beside Diablo's stall, disoriented or overcome by smoke?

Tate's heart raced, his pulse thrumming against his ears, almost drowning out the roar of the fire and the screams of the remaining horse. The building wouldn't last much longer. Soon the roof would cave and everything left inside would be consumed by flames.

Where was she? He ducked low and moved toward Diablo's stall where he'd last seen Sylvia. The crazy lady should have stayed in the house. He and C.W. were the only ones who should have even attempted entering the barn.

What if she'd succumbed to the smoke? He might never find her.

He coughed, pulling his shirt up over his mouth, ducking lower until he was on his knees. The scrape of metal against metal made him turn toward the last stall in the building. Surely she hadn't gone deeper.

Tate felt his way along the row of stalls, closing the doors and counting as he went to give him a frame of reference and a clear exit through the murky darkness. When he reached the last stall, he bumped into a lump on the floor.

"Sylvia?"

A cough and then the raspy words came to him through the smoke, "Oh, thank God." She threw herself into his arms. "The horse won't come out."

"I'll get her. You need to get out of here, now." He pushed the hair out of her face and shoved her closer to the ground. "Crawl, the smoke's getting too dense."

"Which way?" She coughed again.

"Feel your way along the stalls and eventually, you'll make your way to the entrance. Hurry!" He gave her a gentle nudge.

Sylvia stayed put. "What about you?"

"I'll get there before you. With the horse. Now, go!"

This time she moved, crawling as fast as she could, her form swallowed by the smoke.

With his shirt up over his nose and mouth, his eyes stinging so badly he couldn't see, Tate waved his hands in front of him until he found the horse backed against the very back of the stall, quivering and crazed.

It took him several precious seconds to locate the lead rope, but once he had it, he didn't waste time getting the horse out of the stall. After several convincing jerks, the horse followed, swinging side to side, twisting Tate around in the process.

Thinking himself in the middle of the barn, Tate wasn't certain of his directions. The horse had twisted around so much, he'd lost his bearings. The fire had consumed the loft full of hay and flames licked along the walls of dry lumber.

A loud crack shook the structure and a huge beam crashed through the upper flooring, sending sparks and planks flying.

The horse reared and jerked the rope out of Tate's hand, racing away into the smoke. Another beam fell from the ceiling. Tate threw himself into a stall before the ancient timber slammed into a wall, sending a shower of splinters, sparks and flames in every direction. The stall held the weight for only a second, then the door popped off its hinges and the enclosure caved.

Too late to move out of the way, Tate tucked his head and rolled to the side, but the stall door landed on his legs, trapping him beneath. The horse was on her own now. Tate had bigger problems.

His lungs burned, starving for clean, fresh air. He pushed and shoved at the heavy wood-and-iron door, managing to free one leg. But the smoke was getting to him. Then he saw movement through the smoke.

A small figure stumbled toward him. "Tate!"

"Sylvia?"

She bent low and shoved at the door lying over his leg, making little progress. After a few useless seconds, she groped in the dark until she found a charred two-by-four and shoved it under the door, leveraging the wood structure up and off Tate's legs.

"Give me your hand!" Sylvia shouted, holding out her slim arm, her entire body covered in soot and ash.

He held out his hand to her and let her pull him to his feet. Then they were running for the barn door, all the fury of hell on their heels.

As they cleared the door the entire roof caved in a billowing belch of soot and ash. Beams, timbers, splintered boards, sparks and flame shot out in every direction as if a bomb had exploded. The scene was like a flashback of the mortar that had exploded in the middle of the Afghan police compound when Tate and C.W. had served during the war.

Tate scooped Sylvia up in his arms and staggered as far from the smoke and flame as he could. Finally, at a safe distance from the raging inferno, he let her feet drop to the ground. She collapsed to her knees, coughing, and he dropped down beside her, sucking in fresh clean night air as fast as he could between spurts of coughing.

He only gave himself a few moments to rest before he pushed to his feet. When Sylvia tried to rise, he pressed her shoulder. "Rest here. I'll be back."

Exhausted, Tate couldn't stay put, too worried about the rest of his men, now all busy quenching the start-up fires trying to spread to the dry grasses of the pasture. There was nothing they could do now to save the barn, but they couldn't afford to let a grass fire consume the house or the rest of the Vincent Ranch.

Sirens blared in the distance—the volunteer fire department on their way to help douse the flames. Rosa or Maria must have called 9-1-1.

As Tate strode toward the burning hull of what had once been his great-grandfather's barn, a voice cried out from behind him. He turned toward the house.

"Señor Vincent! Señor Vincent! Help! *Madre de Dios!* Help!" Maria, the Vincent's housekeeper, ran across the yard in her bathrobe, her long, gray hair loose and flying about her shoulders.

A cold hand of dread gripped Tate's chest. He found himself running toward the woman, the roaring in his head nothing to do with the fire raging behind him. He caught Maria by the shoulders and held her steady as she dragged in ragged breaths. "Take a deep breath, Maria, and tell me."

She stared up into his eyes, tears running down her face. *"El niño,"* she said, her voice cracking on a sob. "Señor Vincent, Jake. He is gone!"

Chapter Nine

As soon as Sylvia heard Maria's screams, she'd jumped to her feet, her heart slamming against her rib cage. Something besides the fire had upset the housekeeper and Sylvia suspected it involved Jacob. She reached Tate and Maria in time to hear the older woman's announcement.

Jacob had been taken.

The world crashed in around Sylvia. Her head spun, her heart stopping dead in her chest. "No. He can't be gone." She stumbled backward as if in a trance, her eyes wide, her mind a flurry of events playing one after the other, all centered around the cherubic blond angel she'd so nearly reclaimed. She turned and ran toward the house, refusing to believe he could really be gone.

Behind her she heard Tate yell to his foreman, but she didn't stop, she kept running.

How? How could he be gone? Was he lost? Had Rosa taken him? Surely he was sound asleep in his crib, waiting for morning and sunshine to greet him. He couldn't be gone.

Tate Vincent beat her to the door, pushing through ahead of her. He raced to the master suite and through the gaping door.

Two steps behind him, Sylvia jammed a fist to her mouth to keep from crying out.

The crib stood empty, a light blue blanket tossed aside, a stuffed lamb propped in the corner.

Sylvia closed her eyes, pressing a hand to her breaking heart, reliving the day her son was stolen from his stroller in a busy marketplace in Mexico. She'd been the one to be knocked down, helpless to stop the kidnapper from taking her son and disappearing into the crowd.

Rosa sat crumpled on the floor of the closet beside the crib wearing her pajamas, sobbing. She cradled her head in her hands, blood caked on the side of her cheek. "Tate, I didn't see him coming. I should have been ready, but I didn't see him coming." She stared up at him her eyes swollen and red, an angry gash in the dark brown hair, still oozing blood.

Tate knelt beside her and ran his fingers over her, inspecting her for other injuries. "It's okay. No one saw this coming. I shouldn't have left you to fend for him alone."

"But it's my job. I'm trained to protect." Her head sagged forward, her hands dropping to her lap. "I've failed yet again."

"No, Rosa. You didn't fail. Someone got the better of all of us tonight. The fire was only a diversion. A damned good one, if you ask me. Any broken bones?"

"No."

"You may have a concussion. We have to get you to the hospital."

"No. I have to find Jake." Rosa pushed to her feet, holding on to the edge of the crib.

"No, you don't. If they're still out there, C.W. and the guys will find them." He scooped her into his arms and carried her into the connecting room, laying her softly on the bed.

Maria pushed past Sylvia, crying softly. *"Mija, mi amor."* She carried a bowl of water and a fresh towel. "The EMTs are on their way. I called the sheriff as well. They are setting up road blocks." She set the bowl on the table and grabbed Rosa's hand, patting it fretfully. "You had me so scared, *mija.*"

The younger Hispanic woman pushed Maria's hands away. "Stop treating me like a baby. I failed at my job. Again."

"Rosa, we'll discuss this later. I don't want you out of that bed until a medical professional gives you the okay." Tate stared at Sylvia. *"You.* Come with me."

"Tate!" Rosa sat up straight, pushing her mother's hands aside again. "Be careful. She could have set this whole thing up."

Sylvia shook her head, backing out of the room as Tate advanced on her. "I had nothing to do with this. I just wanted my son back. I would never put him in danger. You have to believe me."

Tate shut the door behind him, grabbed her wrist and marched her toward his office.

Try as she might, she couldn't shake off his grip. "Let go of me. I tell you I didn't stage this. I'm not a criminal. I'm a mother searching for my son. My son, who is now lost to me again! Good God!" Her vision blurred and she stumbled, dropping to her knees.

Tate jerked her back to her feet, dragging her into his office where he shut the door. "Jake's my son and I want him back." Not until then did he let go of her hand. "What do you want? Money?" He jerked a checkbook out of the top drawer of his desk and opened it, grabbing a pen. "How much?"

Rage flamed through her faster than the fire had spread in the barn. Despite nearly dying in that fire. Despite the raspy way her lungs felt from all the smoke she'd inhaled, she felt a surge of adrenaline so strong, she had to move.

Sylvia stalked across the room, stood directly in front of Tate and slapped his face as hard as she could.

Her hand stung and she nearly doubled over from the pain.

A bright red handprint marked the spot and twin flags of mottled scarlet stained his high, tanned cheekbones.

"I don't want your damned money," she said, her voice low and gravelly. "I don't want your damned land. I don't want you." She breathed in and breathed out, her chest rising and falling in a measured attempt to calm the anger burning inside. "I only want my son."

"How do I know you didn't set that fire in the barn to distract us?"

"I didn't."

"Rosa's right. Everything was fine until you showed up. How do you explain all that?"

"I don't have to explain myself. I'm here because this is where the trail led to my son."

"I don't believe you. I think you're a lying bit—"

Sylvia's hand swung up to slap him again, only this time he was ready and caught her wrist before it connected.

"Don't do that again."

"Don't accuse me of something I didn't do."

He stared at her long and hard, his grip bruising her wrist.

She didn't flinch—didn't blink—just stared back, holding her ground, the truth her only ally.

Finally, he loosened his grip on her wrist and pulled

it down by her side, still not releasing her. "I'm not sure who to believe."

"That's *your* problem." She wiggled her hand, trying to break free. "Let me go. I have to find my son. The longer we wait, the farther away the kidnapper gets. I love my son even if you don't."

He twisted her arm behind her, dragging her against him, crushing her chest into his. "I love Jake more than life itself. He's my reason for living."

His move left her breathless, the feel of his body against hers more shocking than his accusations. "Okay, so you love him. What next?"

"We find him."

"Then what are you doing now?"

"Making a mistake," he said, staring down at her, his smoldering dark eyes, burning into hers.

"Then don't."

"For some damned reason, I can't help myself." He lowered his lips to within a breath of hers. "Even when I'm angry at you, you make me crazy, and I don't even know who you are."

Her gaze shifted from his eyes to the lips poised above hers. "Don't do it," she whispered.

"Do what?"

"Do this." She leaned up, pressing her lips to his, which started an avalanche of repercussions neither expected.

He let go of her wrist, his fingers tangling in her hair, dragging her head backward, opening her mouth to his.

His tongue thrust in, claiming hers. He tasted of mint and smoke, his sooty hands now grasping the sides of her face.

She gave as good as she got, hungry for him, despite

all he represented. For now, they stood on a level playing field. Each had lost the child they loved.

After only a second, maybe two, Tate clasped her face between both hands and broke off the kiss. "We have to leave now or we may never find Jake."

Sylvia stared up into his eyes, nodding. "This should never have happened."

"It won't happen again." His words said one thing, the hands still caressing the sides of her face said something else entirely. His thumb rubbed at her cheek. "You're all smoky."

"So are you."

"Thanks for helping save my horses." Those words were the closest she could expect of an apology. Tate Vincent probably wasn't used to having to apologize for anything.

Her lips still tingling from his kiss, Sylvia whispered in a smoke-roughened voice, "Thanks for saving my life."

His hand dropped to his side and he nodded toward the door. "I'll give you ten minutes to shower and get ready, then we're hitting the road."

Sylvia frowned. "Where to?"

"San Antonio."

IN LESS THAN FIVE minutes, Tate had showered, dressed in jeans, a blue chambray shirt and a pair of cowboy boots that weren't covered in soot and ash.

He packed an overnight bag and a couple changes of clothing and stepped out into the hallway.

Sylvia stood there in a filmy white Mexican dress decorated in bright red, orange and pink embroidered flowers Maria had given her, with a wide, bright red belt cinching the excess material in at the waist. She wore a pair of flat thin-strapped sandals on her delicate feet. Her wet hair hung down the middle of her back in a long, thick braided rope. She looked like a little girl playing dress up. But the swell of her breasts beneath the elastic neckline of the dress made a man look twice.

Tate was no different. He'd come up with everything but a bra for her and the tips of her nipples stood at attention, the soft brown aureoles showing through the thick cotton.

His stare must have rested there too long.

Sylvia's arms crossed over her chest, a frown twisting her brows together. "Ready?"

He cleared his throat and pulled his gaze back to her eyes. "Let's go."

Rosa stood in the doorway to her bedroom, pressing a hand to her head, wincing. "Keep in touch, boss man. As soon as I can stand without swaying, I'm right behind you."

"Not without the doctor's permission. I have enough to worry about without worrying about you, too."

Her frown deepened.

"Help C.W. figure out what happened here, then we can discuss your next move."

"Yes, sir."

He strode to her and took her arms. "You did more than was expected of you. And I'm not even paying you hazardous duty pay."

Rosa smiled crookedly. "Who would have thought taking care of an infant would be hazardous duty?"

"You should know better around here."

"Yeah. I remember following around behind you as a kid. Everywhere you went trouble followed. I don't know why us being adults would make it any different." She nodded toward the door. "Get going. I want the little guy back as much as you do."

Tate didn't remind Rosa that even if they found Jake that he might not be coming home with them. He might be going home with Sylvia. If she truly was the boy's mother.

First things first.

Find Jake.

C.W. had pulled Tate's truck around to the front of the house and parked it there. He was climbing out as Tate and Sylvia stepped out on the porch. "Again, I saw signs of an ATV, but they were smart and got out before anyone could catch them. Same MO. ATV to a cut fence, loaded into a truck and gone. They were prepared."

"And we weren't." Tate shook his head. "I expected a full-on attack. Never thought they'd create a diversion. We're dealing with someone with a few brains."

C.W. nodded toward Tate's bag. "Going some-where?"

"San Antonio."

"I'm coming with you," C.W. stated, a stubborn look on his face.

Tate shook his head. "You can't. I need someone I can trust here. I'm not convinced Rosa's in any shape to hold down the fort yet. She suffered a concussion and refuses to go to the hospital."

"As thickheaded as she is, I'm surprised they didn't have to hit her a couple times. Guess we're lucky they didn't." C.W. stared at the windows behind Tate as if he could see inside to the woman in question. Although he joked, the tightness of his lips gave lie to his humor. He cared about Rosa. More than either of them would admit.

"Give her at least a day under a doctor's supervision

and you can join us in San Antonio. She'll want to follow sooner. Sit on her if you have to."

"Will do." His brows drew together. "Tate, I don't like you going off by yourself. We look out for each other. We've been doing that since Afghanistan."

"C.W.," Tate said, his tone low and steady, "I need you here for now. Rosa needs you here. We need to make sense of the barn burning and see what evidence they find from the break-in and kidnapping. They might even call here demanding a ransom. I need you and Rosa to handle this end of it for now."

C.W.'s jaw tightened, his fists clenching and releasing. He was still covered in ash and soot from the fire. The rest of the ranch hands worked alongside the volunteer firefighters to keep the fire from spreading. The EMTs treated the wounded and one had been in to see to Rosa.

"I'm not needed here," Tate said. "Jake needs me."

"I can help." C.W. gave one last try.

"Sylvia has contacts in San Antonio. We'll find him."

"What about backup?"

"I promise, I'll keep in touch."

"Don't go in guns a-blazing. You aren't John Wayne and this isn't a movie script."

Tate chuckled. C.W. had used the same words on an operation they'd conducted in Afghanistan, right before they'd busted into a home filled with stolen weapons and rebel fighters. They'd been lucky that night. They hadn't lost a single man. Because they'd all looked out for each other.

"I know the value of teamwork, C.W. I'm counting on you to get things squared away pretty quickly and join me as soon as you can."

C.W. nodded. His mouth pressed into a thin line. He glared at Sylvia. "Don't mess with my man Tate."

She planted her hands on her hips and glared back at C.W. "You know, I'm just a little tired of everyone thinking I'm the bad guy here." Then she sighed, her shoulders sagging. "Rest assured, Tate's calling all the shots for now."

"Keep it that way and you'll stay alive." C.W. glanced toward the still-smoldering barn. "I better get back to it. The fire chief said he smelled gasoline. I'm not surprised."

Tate hooked Sylvia's elbow and led her toward his truck. "Come on, we have to find Jake. I have a feeling the guys we're dealing with will make it difficult."

"You think?" Sylvia said, her voice dripping with sarcasm. "I've spent the past six months searching for my son. Let me tell ya, it hasn't been a cakewalk."

As Sylvia climbed into the truck, she sucked in a deep breath and exhaled slowly, refusing to let depression hit her hard enough to bring her down. After finally finding Jacob, to have him stolen again was more than she could handle. The culmination of six months work had gone up in smoke.

She sat beside Tate in the cab of the pickup, staring straight ahead, wondering where to begin.

"We'll find him." Tate's voice filled the darkness, warming the cold places in Sylvia's heart.

"Do you finally believe me?"

For a long moment, silence reigned.

Sylvia stole a glance at Tate's profile, his square jaw and strong chin a sharp contrast to the fullness of his lips. His eyes stared straight ahead at the road illuminated by the truck's headlights, giving away nothing of the thoughts churning in his head. Only the muscle twitching in the side of his face gave any indication that tonight's fiasco had any impact on him. Sylvia waited quietly, determined that he answer her question one way or the other. As long as he told the truth.

At last he faced her briefly, returning his focus to the road ahead. "I think I've believed you from the start. I just didn't want to admit that I could lose Jake."

She let go of the breath she'd been holding. For a long moment she remained silent, the relief that someone believed her almost overwhelming. For so long she'd struggled to get anyone to take her seriously. She'd fought the battle alone with only her few contacts she'd made during her investigation into gang warfare in San Antonio. Had the kidnappers gone anywhere else besides San Antonio, Jacob could have been lost to her forever.

The hollowness in her gut came with physical pain. "We have to get Jacob back." As soon as she said the words aloud, it dawned on her that she'd used the word *we*. Jacob was her son. When the DNA results came in, Tate Vincent would have no claim to the child. She cast a glance at Tate.

His hands gripped the steering wheel so tightly his knuckles turned white. His jaw could have been carved in granite. "We will get Jake back."

"And then what?" She couldn't help it. She had to know his intentions.

"We'll take it one step at a time."

Sylvia had to be satisfied with that. They had to concentrate on what was most important at the moment. And that was getting to Jacob before something dreadful happened to him. She refused to think anyone would hurt a harmless baby. She'd had to believe that all along or she'd have been a basket case.

"Who in San Antonio did you talk to that gave you

the information about Beth Kirksey?" Tate asked, all business now.

With a deep breath, Sylvia shoved thoughts of a confused Jacob crying in the night from her mind and slipped back into the role of investigative reporter. The only role she'd known for the past six months. "I went undercover dressed as a hooker and walked the streets downtown, asking questions."

Tate frowned over at her. "Wasn't that dangerous?"

"Yeah. I had to hide a few times from pimps, but I knew I was on the right track. I just had to ask the right questions.

"I started telling the prostitutes I was pregnant and did they know of an adoption agency or a couple who would pay for my baby. That's when I found Velvet, a friend of Bunny's."

"Do you think you can find this Velvet woman again?"

"Yeah. But she might not talk to me."

"Why?"

"It was after I talked to her that Bunny was killed in a hit-and-run accident."

"How were you able to track Jake if Bunny...Beth wasn't talking?"

"I went to the courthouse and looked through the adoption records and birth certificates. That's when I found you."

"Do you think Velvet would know the men Beth worked with?"

"I don't know. But I'm guessing that she and Beth had the same pimp. He'd be the one who might know who to contact for selling a baby."

"Why do you say that?"

"Most of the prostitutes are under the protection of a

pimp." Sylvia snorted softly. "And I use the word *protection* loosely. It's more like they're under the *control* of a pimp. Anything they want to do has to go through the pimp to be approved. If Beth wanted to sell her baby, I'd bet good money she went through her pimp to do it."

"Sounds like you know your stuff. How did you survive in their territory?"

"I kept thinking about Jacob. Between dodging pimps, undercover cops and amorous johns, I had my work cut out for me."

"Didn't the prostitutes suspect you?" He looked over at her. "I mean, if you weren't taking on clients, how did you convince them you were the real deal?"

Sylvia smiled in the darkness. "I had my own 'clients' pick me up and take me away for several hours, then I'd have them drop me off again on the same street corner."

"You took money for sex?"

Her lips twisted into a wry grin and she shot a "get real" look at Tate. "No. I wasn't that desperate for money then. I called in a few favors and also paid money for a ride from some of my contacts to and from a restaurant."

Tate's lips curled upward. "Clever."

They sat in silence, watching the miles slide away. Sylvia didn't realize she'd fallen asleep until she awoke to the bright streetlights shining down through her window.

She stretched and yawned. "Where are we?"

"San Antonio."

A glance at the clock on the dash left her disappointed. "It's too late to hit the streets, most of the ladies will be either occupied or home for the rest of what's left of the night."

The darkness of night faded into a battleship-gray predawn light.

"Let's find a room to sleep for a while." Tate ran a hand through his hair. "I'm beat."

"Make it off the beaten path. Out here on the edge of town would be best."

"Done." He pulled into the nearest economy hotel and slid out of the truck. "I'll be back."

Sylvia breathed a sigh that he hadn't insisted on her coming in. She had drained her savings, and the lack of paying work and her recent loss of anything left of value in the car fire had left her penniless. A man like Tate Vincent with all the wealth at his disposal wouldn't understand how low she'd sunk.

Speak of the devil, he exited the motel with an envelope, probably containing a room key card. He climbed in and drove the vehicle around the back of the building and parked.

Sylvia braced herself for what was to come.

"Come on, I could use a couple hours of sleep."

"You do that." It was one thing to accept a room in his house, another for him to pay for a motel room for her. "I'm not sleepy," she lied.

"Yeah, that's why you slept for the last hour."

"That's right. I feel refreshed." She pushed her hair behind her ears and opened her eyes wider, faking being alert and ready to go when every muscle and nerve in her body begged for another four hours of shut-eye.

"I hope you're a better liar when we meet up with the ladies of the night later on this evening." He climbed down from the truck and walked around to the passenger side to open her door. "Out."

"No, really. I don't need sleep. I once went three days

without sleep when working a piece on the effects of sleep deprivation."

"Yeah, and I'll bet you didn't have a barn burn down on top of you back then." He held out his hand. "Come on. I'm dead on my feet."

"You go. I'll stand guard on your truck to make sure no one takes it."

"No way. You're sleeping in the room, in a bed. It'll be daylight soon and this truck can get awfully damned hot once the sun beats down on it."

"I'll roll a window down. I'll be just fine."

His jaw tightened. "You're staying in the room." He reached for her hand.

She evaded. "No, I'm not."

"Why?"

With her arms crossed over her chest, she stayed put in the truck seat. "Because."

Tate sucked in a deep breath and let it out. "That's not a reason."

"I don't have to explain myself to you."

"Fine. Have it your way." He turned to leave her.

Sylvia startled when he spun around, reached in and grabbed her, slinging her over his shoulder like a bag of potatoes.

Sylvia landed with an *oomph,* all the breath knocked out of her for a split second. Then she sucked in air and squealed, "Put me down, you Neanderthal!"

"Shh! Be quiet or you'll wake everyone up."

"I don't need you to carry me into the room. I was perfectly happy to sleep in the truck."

"Not an option. And ha! You said sleep. I knew you weren't as wide-awake as you claimed."

"I am now." She pounded his back.

Tate marched toward a room on the back corner,

shifting her weight so that he could use one hand to slide the key card into the lock. The light on the lock blinked green and he pushed the door open, carrying her inside.

"I can't stay in here."

He dropped her onto the king-size bed, his hair mussed, but he wasn't breathing hard at all. "Again, I ask why?"

Flustered from being that close to him in a very intimate position, Sylvia couldn't think fast enough to come up with a lie. "I can't afford it."

Tate's black brows scrunched together. "Can't afford it? Did I ask you to pay for the room?"

"No. But I will. As soon as I can." Whenever that might be. She'd have to get some real paying jobs and quickly. As soon as she found Jacob and got him back. But every day she searched cost money, something she was fresh out of. Never in her life had she relied on charity, not even after her parents died.

The magnitude of her predicament overwhelmed her. "I can't take your charity."

"Charity? You think this is charity?" Tate threw his hands in the air. "All this fuss because of a motel room?" He dropped onto the bed beside her and flopped back, his booted feet hanging off the end of the mattress. "I'm so tired I can't even think straight. Having you in this room is not a matter of charity. I want to keep an eye on you and this was the only way I knew how."

Sylvia sat up and glared down at him. "Is that it? You still don't trust me? I thought you believed me. Was that all a lie?"

Tate groaned. "I'm too tired to argue. You're welcome to continue if you want. Sleep in the truck, sleep on the bed, anywhere you want. Just let me get a few minutes rest." He lay with his eyes closed, a hand draped over his face.

Indignation melted away as she studied the lines around his mouth and the dull color of his skin. He did look tired and she'd done nothing but argue with him for the past fifteen minutes.

Guilt made her suck it up and stay put when she wanted to go back out to the truck. Being in a room with Tate Vincent could be dangerous. Especially when the only substantial piece of furniture was a bed.

When he didn't stir to take off his boots, Sylvia relaxed a little.

She didn't know if she was mad or relieved that it wasn't a case of charity but one of lack of trust. Just when she thought she had Tate Vincent all figured out, he opened his mouth and surprised her all over again.

His chest moved up and down in a slow, steady rhythm. Had he fallen asleep that fast? She leaned close to look beneath his arm to see if his eyes were open.

Closed.

For all appearances, Tate Vincent was fast asleep.

If she wanted, she could leave him now and strike out on her own to find Jacob. She'd been doing it for so long, it made sense. Besides, Tate might slow her down. This was her chance.

Sylvia stared at him another minute and made her decision. The boots had to come off.

Chapter Ten

Tate woke to muted light peeking around the edges of the heavy curtain. He didn't recognize his surroundings. It took a full fifteen seconds before all the events of the past twenty-four hours flooded in. The appearance of the blond-haired, blue-eyed beauty claiming to be Jake's mother, the car fire, the shooting and the barn fire.

No wonder he'd slept so soundly. It was a wonder he didn't sleep until Sunday. Movement against his side brought him fully alert. A slim, pale hand slid across his chest, resting over his heart. The woman at the root of all things gone wrong in his life over the last day lay snuggled against him, a bare leg slung over his, her white Mexican dress rumpled halfway up her thigh, exposing an amazing amount of pale skin.

His groin tightened, his hand reaching for hers. A groan rose up in his throat at the feel of her skin against his. How could a woman who appeared so slim and delicate carry the burden she'd carried for the past six months? Alone.

As much as he wanted to hate her for threatening to take Jake away from him, Tate couldn't. Instead he wanted to protect her, to right all the wrongs and return her son to her, even if it meant he'd lose Jake forever.

His fingers stroked hers. Her head lay in the crook of

his arm, her breath warm against his shirt. What would it feel like to lie naked with her? Would the rest of her body be as soft and smooth?

The fly on his jeans grew uncomfortably tighter. He should be ashamed of the lusty thoughts he was having toward a woman he'd only met the day before. A woman who could have orchestrated this entire situation to get him alone and make him... What? Aroused?

"Mmm..." Her soft hum did nothing to still his rapidly increasing pulse. Her arm smoothed down over his chest, inching lower until it bumped against the rising seam of his jeans.

The groan he'd suppressed rose again in his throat and he couldn't contain it.

Sylvia's baby blues opened, her full, thick lashes fluttering until she stared up into his face and blinked sleepily. "What...?" Her leg stiffened against his.

"Shh. Be still."

"But..."

"You were tired. I make a good pillow and you've only been asleep for a couple hours. Now, go back to sleep."

Her lashes drifted closed. "But I don't know you."

"Then we're even."

"We shouldn't be this—" she yawned into his shirt "—close." But she didn't move her leg from his nor did she shift her arm higher. Her hand lay within an inch of Tate's growing erection.

He wondered how long he could lie still and hold his breath. Because that was the only way he could keep her there in his arms without making a move. What shocked him most was that he wanted her there. Her soft curves and braless breasts fit against him perfectly.

With more effort than he thought he could muster, he tried to relax and go back to sleep, but he couldn't.

His hand slid down to cover hers, stroking it as it moved lower.

Oh, Lord help him. She touched him there, lighting his entire body on fire. No way he could lay still and not react to her nearness. Her skin alone ignited a flame in his loins, making him want to strip off his clothes and bury himself inside her.

Her hand closed around the ridge, smoothing over it, pressing into the denim.

"Are you awake? Do you have any idea what you're doing to me?" he whispered, begging her to quit at the same time wishing she wouldn't.

After a long, lung-arresting moment, she answered, her breathy voice blowing warm air against his sensitized neck. "I'm awake."

The long, naked limb draped over his thigh tightened, bringing her closer until the warmth at the apex of her thighs straddled his trapped leg. Her dress rode higher until he could see that she wasn't wearing panties, the bare, white skin of her rounded bottom teasing him from beneath the dress. Apparently, underwear had been forgotten when Rosa brought clothes for Sylvia to wear. Not that he minded.

Far from it. But he might regret it later. He found it incredibly hard to see or think past the hand on his crotch.

"Do you know what you're doing?" he repeated through his clenched teeth.

"No, I don't know what I'm doing." She laughed into his neck. "But it's becoming more obvious as we go." She smoothed her fingers lower to cup him.

He grabbed her hand and held it still. "I don't expect payment for the room, if that's what this is." His words were steely, more harsh than he'd wanted to sound, but he had to say it.

Sylvia's body stiffened. "It's not," she said, her voice tight.

"Then why?"

"I told you, I don't know. Why did we kiss in the garden? Why have I been lying here half-awake imagining the possibilities for the past thirty minutes?" She sighed and squeezed him gently. "I don't know. Because it feels right?"

As the pressure increased on him he sucked in a deep breath and let it out. Then he flipped her over on her back and pinned her to the mattress, straddling her hips, holding her hands high above her head.

"Don't mess with me, Sylvia Michaels. I don't take kindly to being led on."

Her eyes wide, her lips soft and full, she stared back at him. "I'm not making any promises. I've been in a failed marriage. I'm not looking for happily ever after."

"Then what are you looking for?" he demanded, the answer more important to him than he'd ever admit.

"I don't know." She stared up at him, tears trembling on the ends of her lashes. "I don't know. I'm just tired of being alone." A single tear slid down the side of her cheek.

Had she lied to him, had she screamed at him to make love to her, he might have taken a step back and let her go. But the one tear and the admission that she didn't know what she wanted from him made him want her more. Damn her!

His mouth claimed hers, his hand loosening its grip on hers, cupped her cheek, holding her steady as he drank from her lips. She reached between them to flick the buttons open on his jeans, circling him with her fingertips, easing him out of the denim.

Tate groaned into her mouth, his tongue circling hers, thrusting deep inside.

In two fluid movements, Tate ripped the belt from Sylvia's waist and the dress up over her head. She lay naked against the sheets, her silky blond hair fanned out against the pillow. She worked the buttons on his shirt while he slipped the jeans down over his hips. "Hey, how did my boots get off?"

Naked, he lay on the bed beside her, and trailed a hand over her collarbone and down over one pale, rosy-brown nipple.

Sylvia shrugged. "I'm not all into that 'cowboys sleeping with their boots' on thing."

"Me, either. Thanks." His lips followed his fingers. He nipped at the nipple closest to him and teased it into a tight peak.

Sylvia squirmed, her fingers digging into his hair. It had been more than a year since she'd made love, the last man her ex-husband. His idea of foreplay was getting her naked in thirty seconds.

"Like that?" Tate asked against her breast.

"Mmm, yes."

He treated the other nipple to the same until both stood at attention, the hardened nubs glistening. Then he moved back up to kiss her, tonguing the line of her lips until she opened to let him in.

"I like the way you taste."

She laughed. "Do you always talk this much when you're…you know."

"Making love?" He nuzzled her neck, his hand drifting down between her breasts toward her belly button. "No. Usually more."

She laughed, her breath catching as he lowered his hand to the juncture of her thighs. How she wanted him to touch her there. Probably more than she wanted to take her next breath.

But his hand paused, the delicious stroking ceasing. He lifted his head and stared down into her eyes. "Do you want more? Or should I stop here?"

She would have laughed if she had enough air in her lungs to make the sound. She sucked in a shaky breath and whispered, "Are you kidding me?"

He shook his head. "I don't make love lightly. And I don't take advantage of women." His voice dropped deeper. "And if she consents, I don't leave her unsatisfied."

Ready to squirm and beg for more, Sylvia's knees drew up and her heels dug into the mattress. She covered his hand with hers and moved it lower. "Does this answer your question?"

He held his hand still, shaking his head. "No. Say it, Sylvia. Tell me what you want."

"Can't you tell?" She stroked his fingers through the moist folds. "What do you want from me?"

"I want to hear you tell me what you want. Hasn't anyone ever asked you?"

She shook her head, the lust and desire swelling deeper. Beyond what she should be feeling for a man she'd only just met. The one she'd told that she wasn't interested in commitment. "I want you to make love to me. I want to feel you inside me. I want you to touch me here." She pressed his fingers inside her channel, swirling them around in the moisture he'd inspired. "I want *you,* Tate Vincent."

He smiled and pressed a kiss to her forehead. "Was that so hard?"

She laughed. "Yes!"

He smoothed a lock of hair out of her eyes and touched a gentle kiss to the tip of her nose. Then his lips descended onto hers.

Miguel had started out a conscientious lover, attempting to do things that brought her to orgasm, but never had he asked her what she liked. He'd always assumed she'd like what he was doing. She'd faked more than once to get through it without making him feel like he'd failed.

Making love to Tate Vincent wasn't just about satisfying him. Just like the way he lived his life, he asked questions and worked hard to determine exactly what it would take to succeed. Even when it came to making love.

And oh, did he have the right technique to bring her with him.

His fingers played magic against her folds, stroking and coaxing her into a heightened state of arousal, flicking against the ultrasensitive nub. Her heels dug into the mattress, lifting her higher, her hand pressing him deeper. When she catapulted over the edge, he moved over her, still stroking her with his hand as he settled his legs between hers.

"Wait!" she gasped. "What about protection?" Even in the moment, she couldn't risk getting pregnant. Not when they were ultimately destined to part.

He held his breath for a moment. "See what you do to me? I almost forgot." While she lay against the sheets in the pulsing aftermath, Tate dove for his jeans, yanking the wallet from the back pocket. He pulled out a foil packet and tore it with his teeth.

"Let me." She took the packet from his fingers and removed the condom from the moist interior, sliding it down over his engorged member. The effort stirred

her, making her want more of what he'd started. She lay
back, guiding him into her, clasping his buttocks in her
hands.

He started out slow, steady, slipping in and out in a
gentle rhythm.

Sylvia didn't want slow and steady, she wanted fast and
furious. She tightened her hands on his butt and slammed
him into her, setting the pace with quick, urgent moves.
Her breathing grew more ragged, her body as slick with
sweat as his. When he came, he pushed into her, burying
himself deep inside, throbbing against her.

She wrapped her legs around his waist and held him
there, loving the way he filled her, stretching her so
tightly with his girth. A woman could get used to making
love to Tate Vincent.

The thought instantly sobered her.

She had no claim on the man. She'd been through
one bad marriage and had no intention of doing that
again. Not that he'd asked. Nor would he. What would a
multimillionaire see in a destitute single mom other than
perhaps her legal claim on the baby he loved? Was that
it? Was this his way of keeping Jake in the family?

Sylvia lay still, Tate still fitting snugly inside her.
Though she wanted to run screaming from the motel
room, she couldn't bring herself to break the connection.
Sure that once she did, it would be for good. There would
be no second chances with Tate Vincent. Not when so
much was at stake.

She needed him only as far as she needed anyone who
could help get her son back. Beyond that, they had nothing in common, no future. Once she had Jacob, they'd
go their separate ways.

But for now, he felt so good, so right inside her.

Tears welled in her eyes. She'd lost so many people

she'd loved. Her parents in a car crash right before her wedding to Miguel. Miguel to his mistresses. And now Jacob. Her son…her only reason for living had disappeared.

She didn't trust herself to love another human being. Not when the stakes were so high. And she had no right to love Tate Vincent. He was way out of her league. Not to mention, she'd barely known him for twenty-four hours.

What would she do when the time came to part ways? She'd cried enough tears to fill Canyon Lake. She had no intention of crying more.

Then why did a tear slip from the corner of her eye?

She brushed it away and moved closer to the warmth of Tate's naked body. A smart woman would get up, get dressed and walk out of the motel room.

Lately, she hadn't been so smart.

And Tate's warmth wrapped her in a security she hadn't felt in a long time. She pressed closer.

His arm tightened around her, his leg draping over hers. "What next?" he whispered into her hair.

Her hand trailed over his chest. "The ladies won't be out until dark. I have no idea how to contact them otherwise."

"Then get some sleep. I have a feeling tonight will be a long night."

Despite the tumble of thoughts churning in her head, Sylvia yawned, her eyes drifting closed. "Okay. But only for a minute."

Tate tugged a blanket up over their naked bodies, settling Sylvia into the crook of his arm. They still maintained that intimate connection and Sylvia didn't want to let go. Not yet. Maybe later.

Tate must have drifted off. When he woke, the clock

on the nightstand flashed a bright green two o'clock in the afternoon. They'd slept a long time. His lungs still ached from all the smoke he'd inhaled, but his head was clear and he knew what had to be done.

They had to find Velvet and her pimp.

Sylvia lay against him, her pale, smooth cheeks rosy from the warmth they generated beneath the blankets. Her long lashes fanned out below her eyes. Blond hair spilled over his shoulder and across the white pillowcases. He hated to wake her. If the situation had been any different, he'd lie there all the rest of the day and into the next night exploring her body and getting to know her better.

He wanted to know this determined young mother. Not just because she claimed to be Jake's mother, but because of all she'd done, all she'd been through on her own. Hopefully there would be time for that later.

Carefully, he slipped his arm from beneath her head and eased out of the bed. Gathering his jeans, he headed for a shower...a cold one. He was ready for a repeat performance from the early-morning lovemaking, but he'd bet money Sylvia would wake up wondering what the hell she'd done. The woman would need some space to digest their actions.

In the shower, he let the water pour down over his heated body. With the stream running down over his face, he didn't hear the door open, nor did he know he wasn't alone until arms circled around him, a slim, naked body pressing against his back.

"Do you always take cold showers in the morning?"

Tate smiled and adjusted the heat on the faucet before he turned in Sylvia's arms. She was one in a million. "Only when I'm trying to make an effort not to scare my partner." He tipped her head up and stared down into eyes so blue he could see the sky in them. "Any regrets?"

"Only one."

His brow tipped upward.

"This place doesn't have conditioner for my hair." She leaned into his chest, her cheeks pink and shiny wet. "Let's not make this a big deal, okay? Whatever happens, happens. No ties, no regrets." She looked up into his eyes, a small frown creasing her forehead. "Deal?"

Tate wasn't so sure about this so-called deal, but he didn't want to chase her off yet. Apparently, this relationship would take some work, if he planned on it being long-term. And she'd made it clear she didn't want long-term.

She'd handed him what every guy dreamed of, a license to enjoy and move on when he wanted. What Sylvia didn't know was that Tate didn't do one-night stands. He didn't take sleeping with a woman lightly and he might just want a long-term relationship.

Sylvia lathered her hands with soap, then ran them over his body, starting at the chest, working her fingers through the smattering of curly hairs, tweaking his hard brown nipples. Her fingers made him nuts. But when they made their way down...

He groaned, his own hands tangling in her long, wet hair, kneading the back of her neck, thumbing the sensitive area beneath her ears.

When she reached his groin, there was no going back. The hard-on he left bed with had gotten stronger. If he didn't have her soon, he'd explode like a teenager.

He relieved her of the soap and started his own attack on her body, sliding suds over her breasts. He let the shower stream over his shoulder to drip off the ends of her nipples. When the soap cleared, he took one of her nipples into his mouth and sucked hard, teasing the tip with his tongue until it hardened into a peak. She had beautiful breasts.

Sylvia arched into him, her leg circling his thigh.

Tate cupped the back of her buttocks and lifted her, wrapping her legs around his waist, easing her down over his erection.

Her quickly indrawn breath was followed by a long, low moan. "God, that feels so good."

"Now who's talking?" he said through gritted teeth as he fought to keep from spilling into her immediately.

"Shut up and move, cowboy." She circled her arms around his neck and lifted herself up his body, then eased down over him again.

"Too slow," he said. Then he turned her back to the shower wall, leveraging her so that he could drive in and out of her, again and again.

She rode him, her head tilted back, her eyes closed, water sliding down her body, her own juices making him slip in and out easily. The pressure built, the heat in the bathroom creating a fog around them, wrapping them in a world of their own.

"Oh, Tate, now. There!" She came down over him, her legs tightening around him as he pumped into her one last time, holding back with every ounce of control he could muster. Then he lifted her off him just in time before he came. He held her close, his body throbbing, the water from the shower cooling him, bringing him back to earth.

Sylvia leaned her forehead into his shoulder and whispered, "Wow."

"Yeah." Tate rubbed a hand down her back and over her smooth, rounded butt. "Wow."

"Thanks." She leaned up on her toes and pressed a

kiss to his chin. "And just remember, no strings, no regrets." Then she stepped out of the shower and closed the curtain behind her.

Tate groaned. Just as Kacee had predicted, Sylvia Michaels was trouble. Just how much trouble was yet to be seen.

Chapter Eleven

"What's the plan for the day?" Dressed in his jeans, shirt and cowboy boots, Tate stood with his hand on the doorknob, looking more damned handsome than a man had a right to look.

Sylvia cinched the belt around her waist, drawing the voluminous Mexican dress in to fit her figure. She struggled to wrap her mind around the fact that she'd made love with multimillionaire Tate Vincent. Not once, which she could have written off as a lapse in judgment, but twice.

Now she could barely face him without blushing. The way they'd scaled the shower walls was…incredible. She should feel ashamed. But she didn't. Making love to a good-looking stranger had taken her mind off all the possible scenarios Jacob could be enduring. Not to mention she'd made it perfectly clear she didn't expect anything and had insisted on no regrets.

She'd do well to take her own advice on the regrets. Pushing her shoulders back, she forced herself to face Tate, his brown-black gaze melting her resolve with just a glance. "I want to touch base with a few of my contacts, and then tonight I walk South Presa Street and see if I can find Velvet."

"I'm not sure I like the idea of you walking the streets like a hooker."

She smiled. "I know what to do."

"I don't know what bothers me more, that you know what to do or that you'll be doing it." His lips twisted into a wickedly stunning half smile. "It's dangerous. Especially now that someone is gunning for you."

No, you're dangerous, Sylvia wanted to say. That smile could send any sane woman over the edge and into his bed. "You don't know that they were shooting at me. They could have been shooting at you." She didn't mention that they might have been gunning for Jacob. And since he'd been stolen, it was more of a possibility than she cared to consider.

The little bit of a smile vanished, replaced by a deep frown, drawing his dark brows together. "I'm coming with you."

"I'm counting on it." She pressed a finger to his chest. "You can be my pimp. We have to make it look as real as possible. Velvet won't buy into it if I'm just hanging out on the corner."

The return of his smile made her heart skip a beat and the butterflies in her stomach take flight. "I like that." The smile faded. "But I don't like the idea of other men groping you."

"Only you?" She grinned. "Don't worry, I have a can of pepper spray…" Sylvia sighed. "I *had* one in my car."

"And the car is toast. I'll get you another one."

"I'll pay you back when this is all over."

"You don't have to pay me back."

She glared at him. "Yes, I do."

He ignored her and continued on. "You'll need clothes to fit the part. I'll cover you on that, as well."

"No."

"You can pay me back. I know, I know."

"As long as you understand. I have just the place to shop for the right stuff." A sly grin stole across her face. "Trust me."

Tate opened the door for her. "I'm not going to like this, am I?"

They spent the next hour in a thrift shop, combing through the shortest skirts, highest heels and skimpiest tops to find the perfect hooker outfit.

While Sylvia sifted through old, new and slightly worn hand-me-downs of questionable taste, Tate stood with his back to the wall, his arms crossed over his chest. Unwilling to try it on for him, she selected what she needed and set it on the counter. She did try on a pair of jeans and regular shirt, something she didn't associate with being in bed with Tate, like the Mexican dress.

Fully transformed in jeans, a simple, white-cotton blouse and a pair of loafers, she stepped out of the dressing room and joined Tate at the counter. The hooker clothes, plus the outfit she had on and a baseball cap cost less than twenty dollars. On the back of the receipt she wrote IOU and signed her name, handing the receipt to Tate.

That she didn't have money of her own made her stomach knot. If it was the last thing she did, she'd pay Tate Vincent back for every dime she owed him. "I don't like being in debt to anyone."

"What's important is that we find Jake. We'll settle up when we do."

Sylvia prided her independence. Miguel had always wanted to provide to the point he didn't want her making any money of her own. To him, it was an affront to his manhood. To her, he'd stolen her independence.

For the first two years of their marriage, Sylvia had placed her career on hold. Until she'd caught Miguel with his mistress, in their bed. Then she'd realized that she had nothing of her own. No income, no job, no parents to fall back on. She'd stuck with the marriage until she'd sold enough articles to fund an apartment and her attorney fees. When the divorce was final, she swore she'd never be in a situation again where she couldn't walk away from it and stand on her own feet.

A relationship should be one where each person came into it because of love and mutual respect and stayed for the same reasons, not because you had no other means to support yourself.

As they settled into Tate's truck, Sylvia drew in a deep breath. "I need you to drop me off on Market Street and go away for a bit."

"What?" Tate had pulled away from the thrift shop and was driving toward downtown. He stopped at a red light and turned to her. "Why?"

"Remember I said I had contacts."

"Yeah."

"My contacts like me to come alone."

Tate's palm hit the steering wheel. "I don't like it."

His concern warmed her insides. How long had it been since someone expressed concern over her well-being? Too long. Yet, she knew she had to do this on her own. "I'll be back, I promise. It's broad daylight, he won't do anything in daylight."

"I don't care—"

"It's the only way I can talk to him." She pulled her hair back, secured it with an elastic band and shoved it into a San Antonio Spurs ball cap.

"Can't you call?"

"No." She placed a hand on his arm. "Please. I know

what I'm doing." She didn't tell him that the street she'd be going to was in one of the most notorious neighborhoods in the city, nor did she tell him that her contact was one of the meanest, baddest gang leaders around. Tate would never let her go if he knew. Every time she'd gone to talk to Juan Vargas, she took her life into her own hands. But she'd learned to never show fear and deal straight with him and she'd be all right.

Tate shook his head. "We should go to the police and let them know what you know."

"These people aren't going to be anywhere on the police radar. They've been in operation for at least six months without being caught. Probably longer." The light changed. "It's green. Turn right and let me off at the next corner."

His hands tightened on the steering wheel until his knuckles turned white. "You can't do this."

When he drove by the spot she'd indicated, Sylvia knew she'd have to make her own move. She waited for another stoplight. When Tate pulled to a stop, she yanked open the door and jumped out.

"Damn it, Sylvia! Get back in this truck!"

"I have my cell phone. I'll call you when I need you to pick me up. If all else fails, meet me at the Alamo in an hour." Then she ran down a one-way street that Tate couldn't turn on and disappeared into an alley.

He'd be mad, but she had to do it this way. Juan wouldn't let her close if he knew she had company with her. Wearing the ball cap low over her brow, she hurried down a side street, away from the fancier businesses and retail shops lining the riverwalk and angled toward the older, seedier residences. Even with the bright Texas sun beating down on her, a chill stole its way across her skin.

The last time she'd been in this neighborhood she'd done the gang violence piece. That story had been in all the Texas newspapers and she'd capitalized on the information to sell it to a magazine. She'd been able to pay off her attorney with the proceeds and had enough left to buy a bed for her apartment. She'd been five months pregnant with Jacob at the time.

Juan had let her slide on a lot of his gang protocol because of her condition, his girlfriend having just delivered a baby girl.

Sylvia wasn't pregnant now. Would Juan be as benevolent? Had he read her articles in the paper or the magazine copy detailing the statistics of gang violence and the behind-the-scenes descriptions of how some of the kids came to join gangs? Was he angry at how she'd described what drove them to do the things they did and the consequences of their associations?

The last time she'd been in San Antonio looking for Jacob, she hadn't bothered to look Juan up. Now she had to rely on all of her contacts, good and bad, in order to find Jacob. Given what had happened to Beth Kirksey, Velvet might not be as forthcoming.

A group of young men wearing baggy jeans, chains hanging from their pockets and T-shirts with scorpions silk-screened across the back loitered in front of a rundown store advertising cigarettes and alcohol.

Sylvia didn't make eye contact, crossing the street to avoid any confrontation with them.

Another block over and one to the left and she'd be at the house where she'd originally met Juan Vargas. God, she hoped he still lived there. She cut through a yard and hurried down a back alley, littered with trash cans and empty beer and liquor bottles.

A burst of laughter made her look back. As she turned

to slip through a gap between two houses, she cast a glance behind her. The group of men she'd bypassed had followed her.

Great. Maybe Tate had the right idea. Going to the police seemed like a much better idea than getting gang-raped in a back alley.

As soon as she rounded the corner of the house, Sylvia broke into a run. One block up on the left was the house she'd been aiming for.

Please, let Juan still live there. Please, let him be home.

The laughter increased and feet pounded on the side-walk behind her.

Sylvia ran for all she was worth, her breathing ragged, fear choking her lungs. She reached the house well before the gang of men came into sight again and pounded on the door. "Please, I must speak with Juan Vargas. Let me in!"

The door remained closed, the windows dark and vacant. The men rounded the corner at a run, laughing and making wolf calls. When they spied her, they slowed, each taking on a cocky swagger.

"Hey, *chica,* want some of this?" One of the young men with a Mohawk haircut pumped his hips at her.

"No, he's a dick. You want a real man." He grabbed his crotch and leered.

Sylvia knocked again, this time in full view of the men. She tried to look casual, not like she was scared, which she was.

"Ain't no one home, little girl. Looks like it's just you, me and *mi amigos.*" The leader of the group, a short, stocky, bald Hispanic man with a scar slashed across his cheek and dragon tattoos covering his arms, neck and the back of his head pushed through the others.

Sylvia stood with her back to the door. She squared her shoulders and, mustering every ounce of courage, faced off with the gang, forcing a nonchalant smirk to her lips. Inside, she wanted to cower, shake and run screaming. "Oh, grow up. I'm not here to provide your entertainment. I'm looking for my friend, Juan Vargas." She hoped the name would inspire fear.

Not a chance.

The leader crossed his arms over his chest. "Señor Vargas is your friend?" He snorted. "Right, and I had dinner with the president last night. If you were a friend of Juan Vargas, you'd know he doesn't live here anymore."

Sylvia's heart sank into her thrift-shop shoes. It was time for desperate measures. "Oh, yeah, then who do you think that is coming down the street now?"

As one, all the young men turned to look behind them.

Sylvia had only this one shot at escape and she took it. She leaped from the porch of the run-down house and ran as fast as she could.

She figured she only had a few steps lead on the men so she had to make it to a busier street and quickly. Never had she been more glad to be in good physical shape. The daily jogging she did paid off. But the men behind her were young, wiry and fast. Faster than she was.

Pounding footsteps sounded behind her, closing in on her rapidly.

She darted between two houses, leaped over a pile of auto parts and vaulted a short chain-link fence. Her heart pounded in her ears, and she couldn't get enough air to fill her lungs, but she had to keep going. If she stopped, it might be the end. These guys might not just want to play with her, they might kill her when they were done. Sylvia couldn't risk that. Not when Jacob was in danger.

If only she could stay ahead of the men long enough to get back to the busier thoroughfares to the streets lined with tourists and security cops.

She darted from between two houses, looking behind her as she ran out into the street. A car honked and brakes squealed as the tattooed man caught her arm and yanked her to a stop.

Sylvia screamed, twisted and fought with all her might. Her foot caught one man in the groin and another in the side of the face. Both growled and lunged at her.

Arms covered in inked dragons wrapped around her and lifted her off her feet. One of the other men yanked off her cap and her hair spilled out.

"*Muy linda.* Look at what we have here." With one hand effortlessly clamping her arms to her side, tattoo man lifted a long lock of hair and ran it through his fingers. "Nice."

Sylvia couldn't believe what was happening or that she'd been stupid enough to get herself in this situation. "You won't get away with it." Good God, it was broad daylight.

He leaned close, his nicotine-tainted breath blowing against her cheek. "And who's going to stop me?"

"I will," a deep, heavily accented voice sounded behind them.

"Señor Vargas." The man Sylvia had kicked in the face backed away several steps, a hand clamped to his bruised cheek, his eyes wide. He slapped the guy next to him and nodded toward the big man advancing on them, surrounded by two even bigger, barrel-chested men with snarls on their faces.

The arms clamped around Sylvia let go so suddenly

she fell to the ground, the gravel on the street cutting into her palms.

When she looked up, she almost laughed hysterically at the sight of a black sedan parked in the middle of the street. Standing with his feet planted wide and his arms crossed over his chest was the man she remembered from her reporting days.

With a jerk of his head, Juan motioned for the two men beside him to step forward.

One on each side of Sylvia, they lifted her as if she weighed nothing.

Vargas's brow rose at the tattooed man. "Ah, Manuel, aren't you on probation? Don't you have community service to perform or something?"

Manuel stood his ground, the other five young thugs crowding in behind him, flipping open knives.

"This is my woman. I hear you've messed with her in any way, I'll cut you down. *Entendido?*"

"She's in our territory. She's fair game."

"Maybe you don't hear so well?" Juan said.

One of the men holding on to Sylvia's arm let go and advanced on Manuel.

The guys behind him moved up to form a single line, all with knives drawn, including a long, wicked blade that appeared in Manuel's hands.

Without so much as a blink, the larger man's hand whipped out, knocked the blade from Manuel's hand. He grabbed the empty hand, twisting Manuel around, jamming his arm up between his shoulder blades.

Manuel yelped, standing on his toes to alleviate the pressure. "I'll kill you, Vargas."

Vargas spit on the ground at Manuel's feet. "You aren't man enough to try." Then he turned away as if unafraid of the remaining gang members.

The man holding Sylvia marched her to the back door of the black sedan, pushing her inside.

Vargas slid in the other side and the doors closed. One of the big bodyguards climbed behind the wheel and pulled the car forward.

The man holding Manuel jerked the arm up higher, then shoved Manuel into his ranks of hoodlums. The tattooed man stumbled, righted himself and spun to face Vargas's bodyguard.

The bodyguard straightened his skin-tight black T-shirt and climbed into the sedan as if he was just stepping out for a Sunday drive.

As they drove away, Sylvia glanced out the rear window.

Manuel rubbed his arm, glaring at the car. The others gathered around, shaking their knives in the air.

"What brings you to my old neighborhood, Señorita Michaels?"

When Sylvia faced Juan, she wondered whether she'd left the frying pan for the fire.

TATE CIRCLED THE STREET twice and expanded the grid, searching for Sylvia. The more he drove the madder he got and the more he worried. He knew the gang activity in San Antonio wasn't so bad during the daylight hours, but as he drove through some of the more derelict streets, his worry intensified.

He checked his watch. Fifteen minutes had passed. If he hadn't found her by now, he doubted he would. Damn her!

With no other options than to wait for her at the Alamo, he drove to the River Center Mall and parked in the parking deck. With time to spare, he walked the short distance to the Alamo and paced outside the ancient mission building, imagining all that could go wrong with Sylvia's plan.

Among the scenarios that came to mind was the one that she'd ditched him to set out on her own. Without her network of contacts and information sources he didn't have much to go on. But he did have friends in important places. You don't become a millionaire without people to help pave the way.

He flipped open his cell phone and dialed Kacee.

"'Bout time you checked in." She answered on the first ring. "Where are you?"

"San Antonio."

A horn honked in the background and Kacee cursed. "Why haven't you called me?"

"Had a lot on my mind. Where are you?"

"On I-35. Traffic's awful as usual. Look, Tate, I'm sorry about Jake and the barn. I've been making calls left and right. The FBI are on it and Sheriff Thompson has promised full cooperation. The insurance adjuster is waiting for the full report from the fire marshal. His preliminary findings indicate that someone set the fire."

Tate's back teeth ground together. He'd figured as much. Still, it made his blood pressure rise to hear his fears confirmed. The barn burning had been a diversion for the real crime. Stealing Jake. "I need Zach's number."

"Hang on."

Tate waited while Kacee, no doubt, juggled her BlackBerry while negotiating traffic to find the number requested.

"Ready?" She gave him the number and Tate committed it to memory. "Why are you calling him?"

"I want the name of Beth Kirksey's attorney and the adoption agency."

"I can get all that for you."

"I'll do it myself. Most likely they're here in San Antonio."

"Anything I can do?" Kacee asked. "I can be there in an hour."

"You'd be speeding." He had enough on his mind with Sylvia, having Kacee riding shotgun would only make it harder. He needed space to think. "Tell C.W. to stay put. I need him at the ranch in case the kidnappers demand a ransom."

"I'll tell him. And Tate…if they do?"

"We'll cross that bridge when we get to it. Later, Kacee."

"Tate, I should be there. There's a lot I can offer."

"I know, but I don't want you involved. I have a feeling this could get more dangerous."

"More than it already has?"

"Exactly. We'll talk later." He hit the off button and dialed Zach Stanford's number.

"Tate! Great to hear from you. How's Jake?"

Zach's casual greeting hit Tate harder than Kacee's condolences. Once again the magnitude of what had happened made the knot in his gut tighten painfully. "Jake's gone."

"What?"

Tate brought Zach up-to-date. "I need the addresses of the attorney and adoption agency Beth Kirksey used ASAP."

"Will do. Give me two minutes and I'll call you right back."

Tate hung up and surveyed Alamo Plaza. Tourists milled about, reading plaques, taking pictures in front of the old mission church and laughed as if they had no cares in the world. The whole time, Tate's stomach roiled and he could barely suppress the anger building inside.

His cell phone rang and he jerked it open. "Yeah."

Zach listed the street addresses of the attorney and the adoption agency as well as their phone numbers. "Anything else I can do for you?"

"Not yet."

"Keep me informed. I'm sorry this had to happen. They were legit as far as I could tell."

"I'm not blaming you, Zach. These people covered all the bases. Now we just have to catch them and find Jake."

After he hung up, he dialed an old friend he'd met in the military. Special Agent Paul Fletcher, currently assigned to the FBI Field Division in San Antonio. Why Tate hadn't called him earlier, he didn't know.

"You've reached the phone of Special Agent Fletcher. I'm currently out of the office. If you have an emergency, contact Agent Bradley." Fletcher's message gave Tate the number for Agent Bradley.

The Austin branch office had sent an FBI agent in response to the kidnapping. Should Tate call Fletcher's backup or not? He didn't want to cause problems between the two offices and slow the investigation.

After waiting another minute and still no sign of Sylvia, Tate placed the call.

"Agent Bradley," a female voice answered.

Tate almost hung up. He knew Fletcher and respected his work. What did he know about this female agent, Bradley? What did it matter, he needed help and maybe Agent Bradley was his man…er, woman.

"Agent Bradley, this is Tate Vincent. I have a situation I hope you can help me with."

"Tate Vincent? As in the multimillionaire Tate Vincent?"

Tate ran a hand through his hair, perspiration building with his impatience. "Yes."

"Paul talks about you all the time. What can I do for you?"

Tate wished Paul had been there to answer his call, but he needed an agent who knew the area and the different criminal factions. "Is there any possibility we could meet?"

"As a matter of fact, my afternoon meeting canceled. Where are you?"

"Standing in front of the Alamo. Can you be here in the next fifteen minutes?"

"I'll be there in ten."

Tate walked the length of the Alamo, along the walls of the ancient convent garden and across the front of the remains of the long barracks. Still no Sylvia or Agent Bradley. He checked his watch. It had only been five minutes since he'd called Bradley and twenty minutes since Sylvia hopped out of his truck.

Five more minutes dragged by and a woman wearing tailored black trousers, black cowboy boots and a white blouse walked across the Alamo Plaza headed directly for him. Young, but not too young, she wore her straight, long, brown hair pulled back in a neat ponytail and a pair of sunglasses hid her eyes. "Tate Vincent?" She held out her hand. "Special Agent Melissa Bradley. What can I do for you?"

Tate shook her hand, surprised at the firm grip and no-nonsense way she got right to business. "My adopted son was kidnapped last night, and I'd hoped you could help me find him."

She frowned. "Sir, have you reported the kidnapping?"

"Yes. He was kidnapped from my ranch in the hill country outside of Austin. The FBI sent an agent from Austin to investigate. But I have reason to believe the kidnapper might be in San Antonio or close by. That's why I'm here."

She removed a notepad and pen from her back pocket. "I'll contact the special agent in charge of the case and see what I can do."

"There's more." He explained how Sylvia played into the events of the previous day. "I'm not sure she's who she says she is, or if my son is her son. But I had a friend of mine on the SAPD check into Ms. Michaels's story. Beth Kirksey is dead. That much is true."

"So you're waiting for this Michaels woman to return now? When did she say?"

"Thirty minutes. That was thirty-five minutes ago."

"Did you consider she might not come back? Do you think she might be in on this whole kidnapping gig?"

"I'm not the one responsible for the kidnapping," a feminine voice said from behind Tate.

He turned, a huge weight lifting from him when he saw her.

Sylvia, her shirt ripped and hair mussed, walked up to Tate and Melissa, her lips pressed in a thin line, her gaze shooting daggers at Tate. "I didn't kidnap my son. But I have a name."

Chapter Twelve

After spending the past thirty minutes wondering if she'd live to see another day, Sylvia hadn't counted on finding Tate discussing her with another woman. Flashbacks of Miguel lying in her bed with his latest love affair made Sylvia's fingers curl into her palms. "Who are you?" she asked, her voice a bit more harsh than she'd intended.

The pretty woman with the light brown hair held out her hand and smiled. "FBI Special Agent Bradley. You can call me Mel."

Despite her gut reaction to seeing the man she'd just slept with talking to another woman, Sylvia couldn't find it in herself to be out-and-out rude. With her son still missing, she needed all the allies she could get. She shook the woman's hand. "Sylvia Michaels."

"Mr. Vincent filled me in on what's gone on in the past twenty-four hours. I'll see if I can pull some strings and get the case assigned to the San Antonio office. I know one of our guys was following a lead on a suspected child abduction ring."

Sylvia's heart skipped a beat, hope swelling in her chest. "You think it might be the same?"

"I don't know, but it's worth a shot."

She placed a hand on the woman's arm. "Jake has

been missing since around two this morning. The more time passes, the farther away he could be taken."

"I'll make sure an Amber Alert was issued and get the department out on the streets checking all their contacts." Melissa faced Sylvia. "You say you have a name? What is it?"

Hesitant to get too many people involved and thus alert the man who could have her child, Sylvia glanced from Melissa to Tate and back.

"Mel comes with a recommendation." Tate hooked an arm around Sylvia's waist. "If you have information, it would be safe with her."

"If you know where this guy is, I don't want a swarm of Feds swooping down on him. He might…dispose of Jacob before anyone gets close."

Mel held up her hand like a boy scout. "I swear, we'll be discreet."

"My contact mentioned the name El Corredor."

Juan had been very concerned about the child abduction ring. His own baby daughter was a prime target for retribution among the gangs. Although he had a tough reputation as a killer and a member of the Mexican mafia, Juan Vargas took his responsibilities as a father seriously and he loved his little daughter enough to tell Sylvia all he knew.

Mel jotted down the name. "I'm going to head back to the office and do some coordinating. I've got your number." She nodded at Tate. "I'll call when I find out something."

As soon as Mel was out of sight, Tate grabbed Sylvia's arms. "Don't ever do that again."

His hands squeezed hard on a bruise she'd acquired from Manuel and she winced. "Ouch."

Tate pushed her short sleeve up and spied the bruise. "Want to tell me what really happened?"

She shrugged his hands off her arms. "No."

Tate closed his eyes, drew in a deep breath and let it out slowly. When he opened his eyes again, he glared down at Sylvia. Oh, yeah, Tate Vincent was ticked off.

Sylvia stepped back. "I had to do it. I needed information and going alone was the only way to get it."

"Who did this to you?" He closed the gap between them and touched her arm, brushing his thumb over the bruise.

"Not the man I went to see."

He reached for her chin and lifted her face until she stared directly into his eyes.

"I know you've been on your own for a while, but you don't have to be anymore. I'm just as concerned about Jake as you are. Let me help."

She laughed shakily. "When you put it that way." Tension drained from her and she leaned into him, resting her face against his chest. It felt good to rely on someone else for a while. Someone as solid and good as Tate Vincent. Not that she'd get used to it. She couldn't. But for the moment...

His hands smoothed over her hair and down her back to rest at her waist. "Did you learn anything other than the name?"

"No." Sylvia pushed away from Tate; despite the heat of the day rising off the concrete, a chill swept over her. "I waited while my contact made calls to several of his people. No one had anything definite. Only the name 'El Corredor.' He did say that I was on the right track to ask the prostitutes. They will know how to get in contact with someone who could hook them up to sell a baby."

"I think we should let the FBI take it from here."

Sylvia shook her head, her fists knotting. "I can't stand by and do nothing. Jacob was so close. I touched him." She looked up at him through watery eyes. "I can't search for another six months. I don't think he has that much time."

"And if I don't help you, you'll go on your own, right?"

She nodded. "I have to."

"Okay, we have until dark. I have the addresses of the adoption agency and Beth's attorney. We should check them out. I gave the names and addresses to Special Agent Bradley. But maybe we can get there before Mel."

Sylvia rolled her shoulders. The lack of sleep and constant worry had her tied in knots. She shoved fatigue aside. "Let's go."

Tate led the way back to the parking garage located at one end of the River Center Mall. Once inside the truck, Sylvia's cell phone rang.

The name "Tony" displayed on the caller ID. Even as it rang, the low battery indicator blinked.

"Tony, make it fast, my battery is about to die," she said into the phone.

"Did you know Rosa Garcia was a highly decorated cop in Austin?"

"I knew."

"She was medically retired after she received a gunshot wound to the leg. No dirt."

Somehow, Sylvia expected this. Rosa's bark was definitely worse than her bite and she had Jake's and Tate's best interests at heart when she'd been nasty to Sylvia.

"Anything else?"

"C. W. Middleton did time in the military, deployed

to Afghanistan three times before getting out. Works for Tate Vincent."

Sylvia avoided looking at Tate. He might not like that she was checking up on his employees. "Anything else?"

"Still checking into Kacee LeBlanc. No police record, but still looking. There's a brother who's done time for drug possession and armed robbery."

"Yeah?"

"I'll let you know more when I know more."

"Thanks, Tony. I owe you."

"You don't owe me nothin'. Just be careful."

Sylvia hung up.

"Who was that?"

"Another one of my contacts."

"Anything?"

She shrugged. "I had him check on a few of your employees."

Tate shot a glance at him. "Which ones?"

"C.W., Rosa and Kacee."

"And?"

"C.W. and Rosa check out."

"They should. I'd bet my life on them."

"I'm sure you did a background check on Kacee before you hired her, didn't you?"

"I did." His gaze narrowed, his finger tightening on the wheel. "And I'm not sure I like where you're going with this."

"Did you know that she has a brother who did time for armed robbery and possession?"

"She told me about her brother in prison. She was very up-front about it. Kacee grew up in a rough neighborhood here in San Antonio. When I interviewed her she laid it all out."

"And you didn't have a problem with a member of her family having served time?"

"I believe in giving people a chance. Besides, it was her brother's crime, not hers."

"Point taken. Do you think it's a bit coincidental that she's from San Antonio and the baby theft ring is here?"

"What are you getting at?"

"I don't know. I'm just thinking we should look at all angles." She sat in silence, mulling over Kacee's family life.

Would the executive assistant to a millionaire put her career and life in jeopardy to get involved with a human trafficking operation?

Sylvia shook her head. "Where are we going first?"

"The adoption agency."

Tate entered the address into his truck's GPS unit. As he drove through the streets, he thought about all that had happened.

The employees Sylvia had mentioned all had a stake in Jake's adoption. C.W. was Jake's godfather. Tate had hired Rosa first to guard over his dying father. When he'd been informed by the adoption service that a baby boy had come available, she'd become the nanny. Nothing in her demeanor indicated any animosity toward the child. In fact, Jake thought the world of her and by all indications, she returned the affection.

As for C.W., what would he gain from Jake's disappearance? C.W. would lay down his life for his friend and Tate would do likewise. As a godfather, he'd sworn he would raise, love and protect Jake as if he were his own.

Kacee had been with Tate for the past three years. She'd been everything to him from secretary, partner and right hand in all his business dealings. She didn't need him for anything, but she still worked for him even after she'd learned all there was to know about Vincent Enterprises.

His assistant had gone so far as to find an adoption agency that specialized in expediency. She'd been just as eager for him to fulfill his father's dying wish as he had been. She'd even offered to be a surrogate mother to his child.

He'd thought that dedication above and beyond, but she'd laughed it off as just part of her commitment to Vincent Enterprises and the boss.

Could she have had anything to do with Jake's disappearance? Tate shook his head. No. He trusted Kacee as much as he trusted Rosa and C.W.

The GPS indicated one more turn and they'd arrive at their destination. "This is it."

Sylvia leaned forward, craning her neck as they passed the address and pulled into the parking space at the side of the building. "Doesn't look as if there are any lights on."

"Not a good sign." Tate turned off the engine and stared at the building in front of him. "This is the place. There were two other cars in the parking lot when I came with Kacee to interview."

"Where did you meet to sign the adoption papers?"

"At my attorney's office in Austin."

"Is that where they handed over Jacob?"

"Yes. Come on." He climbed out of the truck and waited for Sylvia to join him on the sidewalk.

How could things have changed so drastically in the six months since he adopted Jake?

Sylvia tried the front door. "Locked."

Tate peered through a crack in the blinds. "Empty.

No people, no furniture." He looked around. "Someone around here should know when they cleared out."

Sylvia touched his arm and pointed to a beauty salon directly across the street. She looked both ways and crossed, entering the building, a bell ringing over the door.

The strong odor of chemicals stung Tate's nose.

"I'll be with you in a minute," a thin woman with bleached-blond hair called out from the back of the shop where she sprayed water over a woman's hair. She shut off the water, wrapped the customer's hair in a clean white towel and helped her rise from the chair. "What can I do for you two? Haircut? Shampoo?"

Sylvia hooked her arm through Tate's and smiled up at him before she addressed the cosmetologist. "My husband and I were just wondering what happened to the adoption agency that used to be across the street. Have they moved somewhere else?"

The blonde frowned, touching a finger to her chin. "Let's see. Had to be about two months ago. I remember because I had to park in the alley. They had a truck blocking the street for most of the day."

"Any idea where they moved to?"

"I think they went bankrupt. The landlord had to have them evicted." She smiled up at Tate, batting her heavily lined eyelids. "Sure I can't give you a manicure or something?"

Tate noted the way Sylvia's mouth tightened at the woman's blatant flirting. He almost smiled, but didn't. They weren't any closer to finding Jake. "No, thank you." He tugged on Sylvia's arm. "Come on, honey, we'll have to find another agency."

Once outside, they hurried for the truck and climbed in. "Bankrupt, huh? Now what?"

"The attorney."

As Tate pulled out into the street, a dark vehicle raced by. What sounded like an engine backfire blasted the air.

The back window of his pickup exploded, glass flying toward the front.

"Stay down!" Tate punched the accelerator with his foot and raced after the vehicle. "Remember this number."

As he gained on the black car, he shouted out the license plate number. Sylvia repeated it, lifting her head to look ahead.

"Stay down!"

A hand came out the driver's window of the vehicle in front of him with what looked like a gun.

Tate swerved, reaching out to hold Sylvia's head low.

Another bang sounded and the front windshield shattered.

Sharp pain sliced through Tate's left shoulder. He jammed his foot on the brake and skidded to a sideways halt.

The other vehicle shot forward and out of sight.

"Give me your cell phone!" Sylvia held out her hand.

Tate fished in his front pocket and handed her the phone. Not until too late did he realize it had blood on it.

"Oh, my God, you've been hit." Sylvia practically crawled across the console to inspect the wound.

"It's just a flesh wound."

She shot a frown at him. "Just what I don't need, macho bull crap."

"I'm serious." His arms came up around her, settling

her in his lap. "Careful with the knees. The flesh wound I can handle. I don't need more damage to other body parts." He chuckled, liking the feel of her sitting in his lap.

Sylvia's lips twisted into a wry smile. "Okay, it's a flesh wound or you wouldn't be so…eh…flexible." She ripped the tail off her shirt and wadded it into a pad, stuffing it beneath his shirt and pressing hard. "You need to see a doctor."

"You're doing a fine job."

"Infection can kill you if the bullet doesn't."

"Spoken like a true professional. Are you sure you're just a journalist?"

She shook her head and relaxed. "I don't know whether you're joking to keep me from freaking out or if you're delirious."

His smile faded as he stared into her pale, beautiful face. He wanted to kiss the wrinkle from her forehead; he wanted to kiss the worry from her eyes. Hell, he wanted to kiss her in a lot of places. With his truck parked at an awkward angle against the curb, traffic backing up behind him on the narrow street and an interesting woman in his lap, Tate did the only thing he could think to do.

He kissed her.

A horn blared behind them and Sylvia didn't care. Not until a man knocked on the driver's-side window did she come up for air and a sanity check.

"Hey, you two all right in there?" A white-haired man in faded jeans and a short-sleeved cotton shirt leaned close to the window, peering in.

Tate hit the down button on the arm rest and the window slid open. "Yes, we're all right. Had a little trouble, but my partner here is patching me up."

The man gave him a doubtful look that made Sylvia bite down hard on a chuckle.

"Are you sure? That's a lot of blood." He pointed at the spot where Sylvia held her hand to Tate's shoulder. "I could call an ambulance. I got one of those cell phones in my car."

"Not necessary." Tate's hand slipped up Sylvia's thigh to her buttocks. "My partner is a nurse."

"I'll make sure he gets the medical treatment he needs, sir," Sylvia said, fighting back a nervous giggle.

That seemed to satisfy the old guy. "Gotta watch out around here. Been a lot of drive-by shootings." The man's gaze darted around as if another shooter might come along at any moment.

"We noticed." Tate cast a glance at Sylvia. "Thank you for checking on us, but I assure you, we're fine."

The old man climbed back in his vehicle and pulled around the truck, giving them one final long look before leaving.

Sylvia checked beneath the makeshift bandage. The blood flow had slowed. She eased over the console and settled into the seat beside him. "Want me to drive?"

"I've got it."

"Then let's get to the hospital."

"Not until after we check the address of the attorney." Tate bumped over the curb and back into the street, driving with one hand on the steering wheel, the other laying still against the arm rest.

"No. Unless you think that was a random drive-by, someone either followed us or knew where we were going. It's too dangerous."

"If we're in danger, what do you think Jake's chances are?" Tate's question made Sylvia sit back against the seat and stare through the windshield with the bullet hole in it, air rushing in from the shattered back glass.

Jacob.

Dear, sweet Lord, let Jacob be okay.

Much as she wanted to let the powers that be handle everything, she knew they were busy people. Hadn't she run into roadblock after roadblock with the authorities? Hadn't it taken six months for her to get where she was today? "Which way to this attorney's office?"

Across town and outside loop 410, Tate pulled the truck into a small row of office buildings, stopping in front of one marked Hastings, Attorney at Law. "This is the place. Richard Hastings was Beth Kirksey's attorney. He didn't come to the adoption proceedings, but he worked up the papers for Beth and the agency."

The windows were shaded with wooden blinds and the door was a solid mahogany. Sylvia reached for the knob, but the door was already open.

Tate grabbed her and pushed her behind him. "Stay here." He ducked low and slipped inside.

Sylvia waited for two full seconds and couldn't stand the pressure. Following his lead, she ducked low and eased through the door, moving to the side just as Tate had.

Inside, the room was dark, only a lamp in the back office glowed. Coming from afternoon sunlight to a dark interior, it took Sylvia a few moments for her vision to adjust to the limited lighting.

Tate wasn't anywhere to be seen, but she heard movement in the office with the glowing light.

"Sylvia," Tate called out.

"I'm here." She moved toward the sound of his voice.

"You still have my cell phone, don't you?"

"Yes." She fished in her pocket as she moved forward.

"Call Agent Bradley and tell her not to bother to interview Mr. Hastings."

"Why?" As she stepped into the attorney's office, a coppery scent filled her nostrils.

Tate knelt beside the desk.

A pair of shoes was all she could see on the floor behind the desk. Toes up.

Her stomach lurched.

Tate glanced up, his lips tight and gray. "He's dead."

Chapter Thirteen

Sylvia stood on the corner of South Presa and East Nueva streets, desperately trying not to fall out of the impossibly high stiletto heels while keeping an eye out for the black-haired prostitute named Velvet. She'd been standing there since shortly before dark, afraid she'd miss her if she waited too late. After finding Beth Kirksey's attorney dead in his office due to apparent blunt-force trauma to the head, she and Tate spent the next two hours making statements. Sylvia had very little time to change and get in place before sunset.

The last time she'd seen Velvet was on this very corner. She'd had to walk the length of Presa and Alamo streets to find anyone who might know anything about putting babies up for adoption—for a price. With Jacob's life hanging in the balance, Sylvia hoped the search for Velvet wouldn't take as long this time around.

A glance at a recessed doorway half a block down and across the street reassured her that Tate was where he'd promised he'd be, hidden in the shadows.

As usual, a multitude of tourists and employees who worked in the downtown shopping mall and along the riverwalk passed by, stopping at the corners to wait for traffic.

Already her feet hurt and she wondered if she'd be

able to run if the need arose. As far as she knew, Tate hadn't told anyone of their plans. No one would recognize her in the clothes and short red wig Tate had purchased. Squeezed into a bright pink tube top, barely covering her breasts, a short, black leather skirt and the waitress-red stilettos, she looked the part. She even chewed a stick of gum to help calm her nerves.

"Hey, baby, wanna come ride me tonight?" A lanky young man with a shaved head and pimply skin walked up to her.

She crossed her arms over her chest, still self-conscious about the amount of cleavage showing. With a toss of her short red tresses, she stared down her nose at him, giving him her best drop-dead look. "You couldn't afford me, even if I wanted to. And trust me, I don't."

"Don't you give out free samples?"

"Cough up the cash or beat it before my pimp stomps your butt." She stood her ground, aware of movement out of the corner of her eye.

Tate had left the semidarkness of his hiding place, headed her way.

Sylvia held her hand up, just slightly to stop him.

The young man in front of her snorted. "Yeah, whatever. You're not worth it. Why pay when I can get it free from my girlfriend?"

"Lucky girl."

The man left and Sylvia concentrated on the other women hanging out on the street corners. After thirty minutes standing on the concrete sidewalk and flirting with men who slowed to ask how much, Sylvia was ready to find another location for the stakeout.

Kitty-corner from where she stood, a dark sedan dropped a woman off, turned down a side street and parked illegally within sight.

The woman stood with her back to the traffic, straightening her clothing and patting her long, black hair into place before she faced the street.

Velvet.

With her first inclination to dash across the street, Sylvia nearly fell off her heels, stopping her headlong rush. From past experience, she knew that if she wanted information from Velvet, she had to work for it.

A silver Lexus slowed to a stop for a red light in front of Velvet, the driver called out to her. The raven-haired prostitute leaned into the window, smiling and flirting with the occupant, displaying a significant amount of flesh from her low-cut, skin-tight, ribbed-knit shirt.

Trying to appear as if she was already going that direction, Sylvia crossed the street with a group of pedestrians. Now she stood directly across from where Velvet still leaned into the car.

Please don't get in. Please.

The light changed and a car behind the Lexus honked.

Velvet stepped away from the vehicle and waved at the occupant.

Breathing a sigh of relief, Sylvia sauntered across the crosswalk with a mob of one-striper airmen fresh out of basic training and still in uniform.

"Maybe if we all pitch in we can get Robles one of them." One young man with a fine layer of strawberry-blond peach-fuzz across his scalp grinned and nudged his buddy in the gut.

"He wouldn't know what to do with her. Why waste your money on him?" his buddy replied.

"Excuse me, ma'am. How much?" The strawberry-blond airman blushed all the way out to his ears. "I can't believe I just asked that. It's a first."

"Better be careful, Drukowski, next thing you know, you won't be a virgin and you'll be getting a tattoo."

Sylvia winked at the airman. "Get the tattoo, honey."

As she stepped up onto the curb, Velvet gave her a narrow-eyed look. The same look she'd given her the first time she'd spoken to the woman. Only Sylvia had been wearing a brunette wig last time. Would she remember her?

Without looking in Tate's direction, Sylvia had to make it appear as though she was just changing corners, not aiming directly for Velvet. She came to a halt a little more than a yard from the prostitute, strutting the best she could like she knew what she was doing.

"Beat it, this is my territory." Velvet gave a sexy smile to a man driving by with his window down, then shot Sylvia an icy glare.

With a shrug and a smack of her gum, Sylvia said, "It's a free country."

The man whistled, his navy blue Camry creeping by. The cars behind him honked and he sped up.

Velvet glanced behind her at the sedan parked on the side road. The one that had delivered her to the corner. "Look, you're going to make Raul mad. He doesn't like anyone messing with his girls."

Sylvia wanted information and she wasn't going anywhere until she got it. But she couldn't just leap into it without scaring Velvet. "Actually, I was hoping you could help me."

Velvet's eyes narrowed and she stared hard at Sylvia. "Hell, I remember you. Last time I helped you, my friend Bunny died."

Sylvia nodded. "That's right, but I didn't kill her. I didn't even get to talk to her."

Velvet turned away with a snort. "You got her killed by asking too many questions."

"I can't help it. I'm desperate. I…I'm expecting a baby and I need to get rid of it."

With her back still to Sylvia, Velvet waved at a passing car. "Get an abortion."

"I can't do that. I want to put it up for adoption. You know, where the family pays all my expenses until the baby's born." Sylvia struck a pose, still talking away from Velvet, but loud enough the prostitute couldn't help but hear.

"Can't help you." Velvet pushed her hair back over her shoulder and plumped her breasts.

"Bunny did it that way. She got money for her baby. That's all I want, a little help and to get rid of this kid. I never got to talk to Bunny to find out how she got rid of her kid."

Velvet glanced her way, brows raised. "And because of you asking questions, Bunny's dead. You do the math."

"Please." Sylvia moved closer and touched Velvet's arm, all the desperation to save Jacob welling up inside her. "I can't afford to have this baby by myself."

Velvet shook off Sylvia's hand. "Your problem, not mine."

"Velvet, baby, got a problem?" A barrel-chested man with dark hair, even darker eyes and tattoos running up each arm into his shirt sleeves flicked a glowing cigarette butt at Sylvia's feet.

So wrapped up in her conversation with Velvet, Sylvia had forgotten to keep an eye out for the pimp. She assumed this thug with the mean look in his eyes was Velvet's procurer, solicitor, *alcahuete.*

"She was bothering me, Raul," Velvet said. "I didn't ask her to come."

Playing the role of a naive prostitute without a pimp of her own, Sylvia laid a hand on the man's arm. "Maybe you can help me."

His glance roved over her from head to foot. "Maybe. You got no *alcahuete* of your own?"

"No. Mine dumped me when he found out I was pregnant."

Raul brushed her arm off his. "Not interested in someone who's dumb enough to get herself knocked up."

"Look, all I want is to have this baby, give it up for adoption and get back to work."

"Can't help you." Raul hooked Velvet's arm in his grip. "Come on, let's get out of here."

"But I haven't found my mark," Velvet protested.

"We'll find another street." Raul's glance panned the area as if he expected to see someone watching them.

Out of the corner of her vision, Tate, his hands in his jeans pockets, head down, looking like any other man in jeans and a black T-shirt, crossed the street.

Velvet hurried along beside Raul, her high heels slowing her down.

Sylvia ran along behind the man, her feet hurting, making it hard for her to keep up.

Raul and Velvet reached the sedan before she did.

"Please, Raul, I need to know how Bunny did it. Who'd she go to when she was pregnant?"

"I don't know what you're talking about." He fumbled in his pocket for the keys, punched the unlock button and jerked the door open.

Before he could get in, a flash of movement raced by Sylvia.

Tate grabbed Raul's arm, twisted it up and behind him, slamming the pimp's chest into the car door.

"What the hell!" Raul grunted.

Velvet stood by wringing her hands. "Leave him alone."

"Who did Bunny sell her baby to?" Tate slammed the man into the car again.

"I don't know."

"I think you do. I think you sent her to him." Tate leaned close and snarled beside Raul's face. "Give us a name and where he can be found and we'll leave you alone."

"*Madre de Dios,* that hurts," Raul cried, his face contorted.

"Tell me, and I'll make it stop hurting."

"He'll kill me," Raul whimpered.

Tate's voice lowered to an ominous growl. "I'll kill you if you don't tell me."

The anger and steely grit in Tate's tone sent chills down Sylvia's spine.

Raul laughed hysterically. "You won't kill me. You don't have the guts."

"Wanna test that theory?" Tate dragged the man's arm up his back even higher until the man squealed.

"*Madre de Dios!* I'll tell you. I'll tell you!"

Velvet backed away from Raul and the car, her gaze darting left and right.

Before she could make a run for it, Sylvia blocked her path. "You're not going anywhere until we find out where Bunny sold her baby."

"His name is El Corredor." Raul's eyes, wide and wild, darted around the side street, searching every shadow.

"Where can we find him?" Tate persisted.

"You don't find him, he finds you," Velvet said, her tone flat, her face pale beneath the heavy makeup.

"How?" Tate bent the pimp's arm up higher until he was standing on his toes to relieve the pressure.

"Call him," Raul gasped. "The number is in my cell phone under E.C. Call him and he'll arrange a meeting place."

"Get his cell and keys and give them to Pinky here," Tate nodded toward Velvet.

She grabbed the keys off the ground where Raul had dropped them and then dug in Raul's pocket, fishing out a slick black phone. With a little more force than was necessary, she handed them both to Sylvia. "Can I go now?"

Tate loosened his grip on Raul enough that the man could get his feet flat on the ground. "Not yet."

Sylvia scrolled down through the phone's contact list until she found E.C. and hit the call button.

"*Sí.*"

Shock struck her dumb. She hadn't expected to get El Corredor on the first ring. "I have a baby I need to put up for adoption," she blurted out. "How much can you get for me?"

"Where's Raul?"

"He's tied up right now. He told me to call you."

"Let me talk to Raul or this conversation is over."

Sylvia covered the mouthpiece, leaned over and whispered into Tate's ear. "He wants to talk to Raul."

Tate yanked Raul's arm up a little. "Tell him whatever it takes to get him to meet with my girl. Can't afford my girls keeping their stinkin' kids." He grabbed the phone from Sylvia, his voice dropping to a low, dangerous whisper. "Just in case you wondered, I speak fluent Spanish, so don't get stupid on me." Tate held the phone to the man's ear.

"Raul here." He listened for a moment, his gaze capturing Sylvia's. "Yeah, she says she's pregnant." He shrugged. "I don't know, maybe three or four months."

Sylvia held up four fingers.

"Four months," Raul said into the phone. "Yeah, she looks like she's the real deal." The man frowned. "I don't know, ask her when you meet her. Okay…okay…Tower of the Americas in fifteen."

Tate didn't give him a moment to say anything else. He took the phone in his free hand, punched the end button and slipped it into his pocket.

"I did what you wanted," Raul said. "Let me go."

"No." With one hand holding the man's arm up behind his back, Tate grabbed Raul's collar and walked him to the back of the car.

Sylvia unlocked the trunk and lifted the lid.

With a hard shove, Tate dumped Raul in the back with the spare tire.

"Hey! I did everything you asked." Raul grabbed the sides of the trunk and tried to leverage himself out.

"Yeah, but I can't risk you alerting El Corredor that we're coming. Move your hands or lose them."

Raul ducked, jerking his hands back as Tate slammed the trunk shut.

"You can't leave me here, he'll find me." Raul's muffled voice sounded from inside the trunk. "Velvet, get me out of here! Get me out of here, or else."

Sylvia took Velvet's hands. "I'm sorry. I didn't know any other way to do this. Once I've met with El Corredor, I'll drop the keys back by here."

Velvet shrugged. "Whatever." Then she walked to the corner and went back to work as though it was any other workday selling sex for money.

Tate grabbed Sylvia's hand and hurried her away from the car on the deserted side street and toward the Tower of the Americas. "Ready to call in the Feds?"

"No. We have to find Jacob tonight. I'm afraid of what they might do to him."

Tate rounded a corner half a block from the tower and pulled Sylvia into the shadow of a recessed doorway. He gathered her into his arms and held her. "You were amazing out there."

She leaned into his shirt, smelling the fresh scent of soap and man. How she wished all of this danger and deception would end so that she and Jacob could go on living a normal life. On the down side, once it was over, she might never see Tate again.

Her arms went around his waist and she held on tight. For the moment she could pretend he was hers. For a moment she could rely on his strength to see her through the hard times. But only for a moment.

"Let me wait for El Corredor." He smoothed a hand down her back and then tipped her chin up to look down into her eyes. "You stay here."

She stared up into his face, loving how dark he looked in the shadows, how fathomless his eyes were, his voice the only thing grounding her. "I can't. He might not show if I don't go out there. I'm the bait."

"Exactly. I don't like it. Someone killed Bunny to keep her from talking. It could be this El Corredor."

"If I thought there was another way, I'd jump on it. But to get him to come out in the open, he needs to think he's got another woman to use, another baby that can make him money." Sylvia smiled up at him. "I've been at this for a long time. I know how to take care of myself."

Tate's mouth thinned into a straight line. "But you don't have to do it alone this time. Let me help."

"Thanks." She took in a deep breath and let it out, her hands resting on his chest, loving the feel of his solid strength. "You've already helped and you can help again, just by being close by." She lifted his hand and checked his watch. "We should get a move on. I'd like to get there before he does so that he doesn't see you."

"I think we should let the Feds handle this before we get in any deeper."

"We're already in too deep, and time's not on our side. Based on Beth's death and all the attempts on our lives, someone doesn't want others to find out who is responsible for the baby-selling business." She gulped back fear. "And they're willing to kill anyone they see as a threat."

Tate's heart skipped a beat, his chest tightening. Jake was just a baby; he'd done nothing to any of the people responsible for his kidnapping. The child deserved a happy life, with his mother.

Sylvia reached up and touched his cheek. "I'll be okay. Promise."

Chapter Fourteen

Tate captured her hand in his, staring down into light blue eyes he could barely discern in the darkness. "I'm going to hold you to that promise." Somehow this brave woman in front of him had grown on him in the past twenty-four hours. He didn't want anything to happen to her, any more than he wanted anything to happen to Jake. Even if it meant she'd ultimately end up with his son. Sylvia Michaels had been through enough.

With time ticking away and a block to cover, Tate let the world wait around him. He captured her face in his hands and bent to kiss her.

What started as a tender union of lips, exploded into a hot, passionate tangle of tongues. His arms circled her, bringing her as close as he could get her without being naked. Her hands circled his neck, clinging to him as he ravaged her mouth, pushing past her teeth with his tongue, thrusting deep, tasting her as if there would be no tomorrow.

And for both of them, that just might be the case. If anything happened to her on this assignation, Tate would take El Corredor down...or die trying.

They split up in the dark, Sylvia moving ahead to the Tower of the Americas. Tate waited one full minute, keeping her in sight while he checked the Sig Sauer he'd taken from his truck. He gave silent thanks to Kacee for all her nagging. She'd been the one to make sure he'd practiced with it and had it licensed.

Having lived on a ranch all his life, Tate knew his way around rifles and shotguns and the occasional pistol. But Kacee had more than a healthy grasp of the pros and cons of each type of pistol. She claimed her brother taught her everything he knew.

Tate frowned. Kacee hadn't told him that her brother was out. He made a mental note to ask her about it.

He glanced at his watch. One minute. Tate crossed the street, moving among shadows. He half walked, half jogged to keep Sylvia in sight.

She turned down the wide sidewalk leading toward the Tower of the Americas; the tower dwarfed the buildings surrounding it. For a moment, Tate lost sight of her.

His hands fisted and the muscles tightened in preparation for whatever might result from this meeting. When he reached the corner she'd disappeared around, he crossed the street to the side she'd been on and paused.

With a deep breath, he sneaked a peek around the corner.

Sylvia stood on the big concrete plaza in front of the tourist attraction, now closed for the night. Alone and small next to the towering structure, she looked entirely too vulnerable.

From a dark corner, a man emerged, wearing a black jacket, zipped up despite the residual heat from the hot Texas sun radiating off the concrete. A small-brimmed hat provided just enough of a shield to the light that Tate couldn't make out the man's face. But his hands were in his pockets and one of them poked out farther than the other.

A gun?

Blood froze in Tate's veins. What could he do? If he let the man know he was there, he could place Sylvia in more danger than she already was.

Tate tucked his Sig Sauer into his pocket and crept around the plaza to a position behind the man, checking for others as he went.

With her back to the shadows, Sylvia didn't see El Corredor at first. She turned three hundred and sixty degrees, then her body stiffened and her hands dropped to her sides. She and El Corredor were far enough away, Tate could hear their conversation only as a murmur.

He shouldn't have let her go out there alone. The image of Beth Kirksey flashed in his mind. She'd been a down-and-out prostitute, probably desperate for money to fund her next fix. But she hadn't deserved to die.

Sylvia didn't deserve to die. Tate had just straightened to step out of the shadows when a movement behind him told him he wasn't alone.

He spun as a fist came out of nowhere, connecting with his jaw.

The force of the impact toppled Tate onto the pavement. His jaw burning, he rolled and leaped to his feet. The guy was on him before he could raise his hands to protect himself.

A flying foot landed in his gut, blasting the wind out of his lungs. He staggered backward, trying to inhale and failing miserably. The edges of his world faded, but Tate clung to consciousness, knowing he was Sylvia's only hope of staying alive.

His chest eased and he sucked in a breath, raised his arms in time to deflect the next kick, tilted and let loose with a side kick his tae kwan do instructor would have been proud of.

He dropped into a fighting crouch and blocked the

next punch with his uninjured forearm, landing one of his own punches in the man's solar plexus and a quick jab to his kidney.

The man grunted, staggered back a step and came at him like a charging bull, nostrils flared, fists swinging.

Alert now, Tate blocked an uppercut, dodged a right cross and used the man's momentum to jerk him forward, sending a knee to the man's crotch.

The attacker went down, a low agonized groan the only thing rising from the pavement.

Tate kicked him in the kidney and waited for him to get up.

The guy rolled, clutching his privates, unable to move from the fetal position.

A scream drew his attention to where Sylvia had been in the middle of the plaza.

Only she wasn't there anymore. And neither was El Corredor.

Tate had been too busy saving his own skin he'd failed Sylvia. Which way had they gone?

A bright red stiletto lay on the far side of the plaza near a wide sidewalk headed toward the exit of Hemisphere Park.

Tate ran, his breathing ragged, his heart beating erratically. They could veer off at any point and Sylvia would be gone. He nearly missed the second stiletto, almost tripping over it.

They couldn't be far, but Sylvia was running out of clothing to leave as a trail for him to follow.

A faint squeal sounded from ahead.

Tate could see the street ahead, a car pulled up to the curb with El Corredor struggling to shove Sylvia into it.

If he hadn't been so worried about her, he'd have

laughed. Sylvia gave the man hell, biting, kicking and scratching. Her fight bought enough time Tate hoped he could close the gap. He ran full-out, eating up the yards one stride at a time.

"Get in the car, or I'll shoot you," the man said, the gun he'd carried in his pocket now out and in plain sight.

Tate didn't slow down because of the gun. He knew that if Sylvia got in that car, she didn't have a chance. El Corredor would take her somewhere Tate wouldn't be able to find and kill her.

Without thinking, he plowed into the man, jerking his arm upward.

The weapon discharged in the air. The two men slammed against the car, trapping Sylvia beneath them.

Tate held on to the man's wrist, banging it against the roof of the sedan. The man's hat slipped from his head and fell to the ground, exposing dark brown hair.

Sylvia did the best she could to pound against El Corredor's back, her arms too pinned to be of much use.

Throwing his weight to the right, Tate dragged the man with him, freeing Sylvia, but getting himself pinned between the attacker and the car.

Sylvia dropped to the ground and scooted out of range. But not for long.

Tate couldn't see what she was doing until the man wielding the gun jolted against him and Sylvia's head appeared above theirs.

She'd leaped onto the baby trafficker's back and proceeded to pull hard on his hair screaming, "Let him go!"

She wrapped her legs around the guy and refused to let go.

"Get the hell off!" With a woman on his back, a man holding his gun hand high, the man couldn't maintain his balance long.

His feet backed against the curb and he fell, the gun flying from his fingers.

Sylvia jumped free, landing on her hands and knees on the sidewalk a few feet from the man. She scrambled for the weapon.

The baby trafficker rolled to his stomach and reached for her.

Tate dove for El Corredor, straddling him and pinning him to the ground.

As she reached for the gun, the man Tate had been fighting back by the tower appeared and stepped on the weapon, pointing one of his own at Sylvia's head. "Touch it and I'll blow your brains out."

Tate jerked El Corredor's head back by his hair, pulled his gun from his waist band, and stuck it to El Corredor's head. "Hurt her and I'll blow your boss away."

Sylvia stared across the concrete at Tate, her eyes wide, her hands raised in surrender.

The man beneath him lay still for a long moment.

"Well, what's it going to be?" Tate tugged a little harder on the man's hair. "Looks like we have a bit of a standoff here."

"Let her go," El Corredor called out.

The other man didn't move.

"*Mierda!* Let her go!" He rattled off something in Spanish that Tate could barely hear, but he got the gist.

"No, you won't be taking care of her later. If I catch you anywhere near her, I swear I'll kill you," Tate promised. "Now have your amigo throw down his gun."

"Do as he said," El Corredor grunted.

The man frowned, hesitated for what seemed like an eternity, his gun still pointed at Sylvia. Then he tossed the weapon to the ground, out of reach.

Sylvia leaped to her feet and ran to stand behind where Tate had El Corredor pinned to the ground.

"My cell phone is in my back pocket. Call Special Agent Bradley." Tate climbed to his feet, his hand still holding the gun to the man's head.

As Sylvia dug into his back pocket to pull out the cell phone, Tate didn't notice El Corredor kick out until his foot caught Tate's ankle and knocked him off balance.

The henchman dove for his weapon.

Tate straightened in time to fire off a round at the man before he could grab his gun. The bullet ricocheted off the concrete next to the handle.

The tattooed man tripped and hit the ground. He rolled to his feet and took off across the concrete, heading for the safety of a building.

Taking advantage of the distraction, El Corredor dove into the car and slammed the door behind him.

Tate grabbed the door handle, but the door was locked.

The engine revved to life and the car lurched, climbing the curb before spinning out onto the street, leaving a trail of burned rubber half a block long.

Tate stood in the middle of the road, his gun pointed at the retreating vehicle, but he'd already lost his opportunity. They'd lost El Corredor and with him, their only link to the location of the stolen babies.

Sylvia stood beside him, her shoulders slumped, tears poised on the edges of her eyelids. "Now what? We still don't know where Jacob is."

"We'll find him. Let's get back to Velvet and Raul and see if they know anything."

Sylvia walked several steps, turned and walked back. "We have to find Jacob. Now that El Corredor knows we're looking, he'll be even more motivated to do away with the…" Sylvia's voice broke. "Evidence."

"We'll find him."

"How?"

"Let's get to the truck. If Raul's still in the trunk, I'd bet my shirt Velvet is nearby."

"You don't think he's found a way out yet?" Sylvia shook her head.

"If he has, he'd be hiding if he thought El Corredor was after him."

Tate had already thought the same, but he didn't want to make her more depressed than she already was. "You're a fighter, Sylvia. Don't give up now."

She leaned into his shirt, her fingers clutching the material. "Yeah, I have to be strong. But sometimes it's so darned hard."

He held her, stroking her hair down her back, the red wig lost somewhere between here and the Tower of the Americas. He preferred the silky tresses of her hair as it ran through his fingers. "We'll find Jake," he said, his lips against her temple. She smelled of strawberry shampoo, a scent he would forever remember as part of her.

She let him hold her for a minute more, then she pushed away, sucked in a deep breath, her shoulders stiffening. "Okay, then. Let's find Raul and Velvet. I'll bet my pink tube top they know more than they told us."

Tate hoped they did. For Jake's sake.

Sylvia accomplished the walk back to the River Center

Mall parking lot barefoot and in silence. By the time she
climbed into the damaged pickup truck, her entire body
felt as limp as a noodle and beyond exhausted. But she
refused to give up. Jacob was out there somewhere and
she'd find him.

Tate pulled out onto Alamo Street headed south. He
crossed to North Presa and continued moving slowly,
pausing at the street corners.

Sylvia craned her neck, searching for Velvet. She had
to be there somewhere.

Just when she'd given up hope, she spied the raven-
haired woman climbing out of a shiny Acura, straightening her miniskirt.

She waved at the driver and stepped up on the curb.

"Stop!" Sylvia yelled. Even before Tate could pull to
the side of the road, Sylvia had her seat belt off and was
halfway out of the truck, dropping down on the street.
Dodging cars, she crossed to the other side.

Drivers skidded to a halt, horns honking, but Sylvia
didn't care as long as she made it across the street and
caught the only person who might possibly know how
to find her child.

Velvet looked up at the commotion on the street, her
brows rising. When she spotted Sylvia, she turned and
ran.

No. She couldn't get away. Not with so much at stake.
Sylvia ran after her. Barefoot, she easily caught the
woman who still wore her signature stilettos. Her breath
coming in sobbing gasps, she grabbed the only thing she
could reach, Velvet's dark mass of curls, yanking her to
a stop.

"Leave me alone, you witch!" Velvet kicked out
at Sylvia, her sharp-pointed shoes connecting with
Sylvia's shin.

Sylvia yelped but held tight to the wad of hair. "Where do they keep them? Tell me!"

"I don't know what you're talking about." Velvet swung her claws at Sylvia, catching her arm and ripping into her skin. "Let me go."

"Not until you tell me where they keep the babies." She swung around, the force of her movement slinging Velvet off her high-heeled shoes. She fell to the ground.

Sylvia sat on her, pinning her hands beside her head. "My son is one of the babies they stole. I want him back, do you hear me?"

Velvet's eyes widened. "Your son?"

"Yes, my son. They stole him from me last night." Despite her determination to remain angry, Sylvia couldn't stop the flow of tears. "I have to find him. I think they might try to kill him."

All of the fight left Velvet and she lay against the sidewalk looking up at Sylvia. "I'm so sorry. I really don't know where they are. You have to believe me." A tear fell from the corner of her eye, taking with it a trail of eyeliner. "I'd tell you if I did."

The anger left Sylvia, replaced by a hollow, empty feeling of hopelessness. She wanted to beat the answer out of Velvet, but knew it would do no good.

Velvet's sad eyes brimming with tears told it all. She didn't know.

Sylvia climbed to her feet and held out her hand. Velvet took it and allowed Sylvia to help her to her feet. "Here's the key to Raul's car." Sylvia handed her the keys.

"I have to go. Raul will be looking for me." Velvet glanced around. "If I find out anything, how can I let you know?"

Sylvia gave her the number to her cell phone. "I don't have a charger and my battery is low, but I'll check my messages remotely if necessary. Anything you learn… anything…just call me." She held on to Velvet's hands longer than necessary, as if by letting go, she released her last hope of finding Jacob.

"I will. I promise." Velvet grabbed her bright red clutch from where she'd dropped it on the ground, dug out a rhinestone-encrusted cell phone and keyed the number in. After she dropped the phone back into her clutch, she squeezed Sylvia's hand. "Have faith. You'll find him." Then she left Sylvia standing on the sidewalk on Presa Street.

Tate pulled up beside her, having circled around the block with no place to stop and get out.

Sylvia climbed into the truck and slumped into the seat.

"What happened? Did she get away?"

"No. I let her go."

"But she might know where Jake is."

Sylvia shook her head. "No, she doesn't."

"She could be lying."

"No. If she'd known, she would have told me."

"I wish you'd let me ask the questions."

"Why? I would have beat the answers out of her if I thought she had them." Sylvia leaned her head back and rubbed her eyes. "She doesn't know. The only person who knows wouldn't tell us now if his life depended on it."

Tate eased into the traffic and headed for the interstate. Once on it, he floored the accelerator, bringing the truck up to seventy in under ten seconds. "What now?"

"What can we do?"

"We need to tell Melissa what we know and let her handle it."

"I don't think we have any other choice. Short of knocking on every door in the city of San Antonio, we don't have a clue where to start. For all we know, Jacob isn't even in San Antonio." She dropped her hand to her lap and stared down at her fingers. "Poor baby must be terrified."

Tate reached out and took her hand, holding it in his big warm fingers. "Have faith. We'll find him."

She gave a short, mirthless laugh. "That's what Velvet said. I've been looking for so long, I'm beginning to lose faith."

"You found him once, you'll find him again."

"Thanks." Sylvia lifted Tate's hand and pressed it to her cheek, the warmth in the cool interior of the truck seeping into her cold skin. "Right now I could sleep for a hundred years."

Tate pulled off the interstate at the next exit and got a room at a motel.

Sylvia didn't argue when he only got one room, she didn't care anymore. Jacob was lost. Her heart was breaking and she couldn't fight any longer.

"Come on, sweetheart." Tate helped her from the truck, grabbed his gym bag and led the way into the room.

Once inside, he tossed the gym bag to the floor and stood looking at her. "Get a shower. You'll feel better."

"I don't have the energy to move." Sylvia sat on the edge of the bed and buried her face in her hands. "I'm so tired."

"Here." He slipped his hand into hers and dragged her back to her feet. "Let me help." He pulled at the hem of the tube top, dragging it up and over her head. Without a bra, her bare breasts sprang free, the air-conditioning pebbling her nipples.

Despite her lethargy, Sylvia felt a tug low in her belly and warmth spread slowly upward.

Tate turned her around and worked the button on the black, faux-leather skirt. Then the zipper slid down. His hands slipped inside the edges of the skirt and wrapped around her hips. They rounded her belly and sank lower still, cupping the apex of her thighs.

Sylvia leaned back against Tate, absorbing his warmth, letting his strength seep into her.

With slow, deliberate movements, he slid the skirt off, his hands following over her hips, buttocks, down her thighs to her calves, massaging the tense muscles.

The soft pressure of lips pressed to the inside of her thigh.

She shifted, parting her legs, her hands smoothing down over her naked tummy to the mound of hair.

While Tate trailed kisses from the back of her thigh to the swell of her buttocks, Sylvia slid a finger inside her folds, touching that sensitive nub.

Tate rose behind her, his jeans coarse against her naked skin, the hard ridge behind his fly tempting her beyond redemption.

With a deep, tortured breath, she turned in his arms, her breasts rubbing against the cotton fabric of his shirt, deliciously soft.

"For now, make me forget," she whispered. Her hands circled the back of his neck, pulling his face close enough she could kiss him.

He held back. "Only for a moment." Then his lips claimed hers, his tongue pushing past her teeth to twist and taste hers.

Her fingers moved feverishly, tugging at the black

T-shirt, lifting it up and over his head. She needed him to be naked, to feel his skin against hers, to chase away the demons, the doubt, the worry.

Before his shirt hit the floor, she had the button of his jeans open, her hand sliding the zipper downward.

His member sprang free—long, hard and proud.

Sylvia took him in her hand, reveling in the steely strength and the velvety smoothness. Wanting him more than she cared to breathe, she guided him to her.

"No." He pulled free of her touch.

Sylvia looked up into his eyes, unable to process his withdrawal.

He smiled. "Not yet." He bent and lifted her, gently laying her on the comforter, her knees draped over the edge of the bed, her feet dangling toward the floor.

He shed his jeans and stepped between her thighs. Leaning over her, he took one pebbled nipple between his lips, his hands cupping her breasts, massaging them between his fingers.

Inch by excruciating inch, he worked his way down her torso, nibbling, tasting and tempting her to scream with frustration.

When he dropped to his knees, his hands guiding her legs over his shoulders, Tate had her body on fire, aching with the need to consummate their union. She wanted him to drive into her, hard and fast. Tomorrow be damned.

His mouth found her entrance, tracing the dewy dampness upward to her folds, tonguing her until her back arched off the mattress.

Tension built to a sharp crescendo, every nerve centered on one place. Sylvia moaned, the pleasure so intense she thought she might die. Then she plunged over the edge, succumbing to ecstasy, her body jerking with the force.

Only then did Tate rise to his feet, and thrust into her, burying himself, his shaft fully sheathed in her heat. He pumped in and out, his hands steadying her hips.

He filled her, completed her like no one had ever done.

On his final plunge, Sylvia planted her heels and raised her hips, meeting his powerful thrust.

Head thrown back, his chest swelled out, Tate held her hips against him, his member throbbing, pulsing inside of her.

Several breath-stopping minutes passed and the tension drained from Sylvia.

Tate slid her up onto the bed and lay down beside her, gathering her into his arms. They lay together, their limbs intertwined until Tate's belly rumbled.

Sylvia kissed his lips. "You need food and I need a shower."

"I thought you were too tired."

"I was." She kissed him again, loving the stubble of his beard, the scent of male and the hardness of his muscles against her breasts. "Can we call out for pizza?"

"They're probably all closed for the night. I'll go see what I can find close by."

"Good. That'll give me time to shower." She rose from the bed, only mildly modest. After what he'd done to her…after what they'd done together, modesty shouldn't be a factor. But Sylvia had promised no strings.

As Tate lay stretched across the bed, his body a magnificent specimen of the male anatomy, Sylvia felt a stab of regret that she'd made that darned promise. She gathered her clothing and headed for the bathroom.

Tate rose from the bed, slipped into his jeans and

boots. With his shirt in hand, he paused at the door. "I'll be back in just a few minutes. Don't open the door for anyone but me."

"I won't." She hurried into the bathroom, shutting the door behind her.

THE DOOR TO THE MOTEL room opened on squeaking hinges and closed with a solid clunk.

Sylvia leaned against the bathroom door, the smoothly painted wood cool against her naked backside.

Tate had felt so incredibly good inside. He'd been the perfect lover, gently attending to her desires first. Damn, she'd miss him when the time came to leave.

She pulled the shower curtain back, adjusted the water and climbed in, letting the warm spray wash over her.

If only she could wash Tate Vincent out of her system as easily as she washed shampoo out of her hair.

As she stepped from the shower, her cell phone buzzed from the back pocket of her jeans.

Sylvia dug the phone out, her hand shaking. Could it be someone with news of Jacob? Her low battery indicator blinked.

She punched the talk button and pressed the receiver to her ear, her breath lodged in her lungs. "Hello?" She prayed her battery would last just a little longer.

A voice, barely above a whisper spoke into her ear. "It's Velvet. I know where they have your son."

Chapter Fifteen

TATE JUGGLED A BAG of groceries in his hand, digging in his back pocket for the key card.

Sylvia should be out of the shower by now. He'd contacted Melissa while he'd been driving around looking for a twenty-four-hour convenience store. She'd been sleeping, but as soon as she knew who it was, she'd come wide-awake, taking down the information he gave her and asking questions of her own.

She informed Tate that they had an undercover agent working the gang issues. She'd get a message to him to dig around, see if he could discover where they hid the stolen or purchased babies. "Be careful," she'd warned. "The Crips play for keeps. They aren't afraid to kill first, ask questions later."

The key card slid into the door and the light flashed green. Tate pushed through.

The comforter lay just as tumbled as it had when they'd made love. The door to the bathroom stood slightly ajar. "Sylvia?"

Behind him the door swung shut, the lock engaged, echoing off the walls of the tiny room.

What felt like a cold fist squeezed the air out of Tate's lungs.

He dropped the bag of groceries on the dresser and

ran for the bathroom, hitting the door so hard, it bounced off the wall. "Sylvia!"

Steam still fogged the mirror. The clothes she'd taken into the bathroom were gone. The shower stood empty except for the drops of water clinging to the smooth porcelain.

Sylvia was gone.

Tate froze for a moment, no thoughts scrambling in his head, nothing, just emptiness. Then a thousand images crowded in on him. His father riding the fence line; his father lying on the dusty ground, his chest laid open with a knife wound; the first day he'd held Jake, the smile on the golden-haired child's face, the blue eyes staring up at him. Just like his mother's.

Sylvia, whose pale blue eyes mirrored Jake's, whose long blond hair sifted like silk threads through his fingers, whose body completed his.

Gone.

Tate yanked his phone from his back pocket and punched the number Sylvia had given him. The phone rang ten times before a canned greeting answered that the cellular customer was not available.

Was she not answering, or was it that she couldn't answer? She didn't have a way to charge her battery—the phone could have died.

Who could he turn to?

His cell phone rang and he almost dropped it on the bathroom tile.

Kacee LeBlanc displayed on the caller ID.

Tate answered. "Kacee, I need your help."

"What's happening?"

"Sylvia is gone."

"Gone? How? Where?"

Tate pushed a hand through his hair and turned to

face the empty room, the essence of their lovemaking still lingering in the air. "I don't know where she is, I just know I have to find her."

"Hold on, big guy. Everything will be okay. Since you can't find Jake, she's probably skipped out of town. Without the kid, she has nothing to leverage over you."

Tate held the phone away, staring down at it as if it were alien. He placed the receiver to his ear and demanded, "What are you talking about?"

"You know, she was probably going to blackmail you into paying to keep Jake."

"You have no idea what you're talking about. You don't know anything about her."

"And you've only known her for twenty-four hours. What exactly do you know about Sylvia Michaels? Nothing other than the lies she's filled your head with. She's not the mother of your son, Tate. How could you believe her? You were there when Beth Kirksey signed over her child to you."

Tate's teeth ground together. When Kacee got an idea between her teeth, short of yanking it out, teeth and all, she wasn't letting go of it easily. "Just get here."

"And where might *here* be?"

He gave her the name of the motel, then paused. "No, never mind. Call me when you're in San Antonio. We can set up a meeting location."

"Can we meet in ten minutes?"

"It's more than an hour from your place."

"Tate, I'm in San Antonio. That's why I called."

"What the hell are you doing here?"

"Nice that you care," she said, her voice dripping with sarcasm. "I thought I'd pay a visit to a sick friend and while I was at it check in and make sure you don't go off the deep end." She laughed once without a shred of humor in the tone. "Sounds like you might already have. Besides, C.W. was worried about you."

"I can take care of myself."

"Yeah? Then why haven't you answered your phone for the past couple of hours?"

He sucked in a deep breath and let it out. "Again, I can take care of myself."

"Maybe you don't get it, but you're worth millions, Tate Vincent. Anyone with half a brain that recognizes you would be tempted to take you for a ride, maybe hold you hostage to get at all those millions."

"Just meet me here in ten minutes."

"Will do."

As Tate pulled his phone away from his ear, Kacee spoke. "Oh, and Tate?"

"What?"

"Don't fall for her cute little act. That's all it is…an act."

Tate grabbed the groceries, the gym bag he'd tossed on the floor earlier and left the room. Staying there served no purpose and knowing what they'd done in that bed only made him even more angry. He'd wait in the truck before he spent another minute in that room.

His loins ached with the residual reminder of how she'd felt beneath him. With a little more force than was necessary, he threw the gym bag into the backseat of his truck and set the grocery bag down. Then he walked to the lobby and pushed through the glass doors.

The clerk behind the counter smiled a welcome. "May I help you, sir?"

"Did you see a woman leave the parking lot a few minutes ago? Or maybe a car come and go?"

"As matter of fact, I did. A blonde got into a car with someone and they left, just five minutes ago."

"Of her own free will?" Tate asked.

The young man shrugged. "Beats me. She didn't have someone shove her in, if that's what you're asking. She'd been waiting for a minute or two. Pretty blonde." His lips twisted into a grin. "That's why I was watching."

Tate wanted to slam his fist into a wall. "Thanks." He performed an about-face and exited the lobby. So she'd left with someone else. Someone she'd been waiting for. No note, no call, nothing. Damn her!

Kacee's silver Lexus purred into the drive-through in front of the motel and she jumped out. "God, Tate, you don't know how glad I am to see you." She wrapped her arms around his waist and hugged him. "Don't worry, this too will pass. You'll be all right."

"Yeah, but will Jake?" He rested his hands on her waist for a moment, then pushed her to arm's length. "That little guy doesn't know what's going on. He's got to be scared out of his mind."

Kacee leaned back and stared up into Tate's face, shaking her head. "He's gotten under your skin, hasn't he?"

"Damn right, he has."

"I don't know why you didn't just settle down and have a kid of your own." She pushed out of his reach and walked a few steps. "There are plenty of women who'd love to have your baby."

Except one. Sylvia had made it clear that she didn't want a commitment from him. No strings, no promises.

What if he wanted strings, what if he wanted more children? What if he wanted Sylvia in his life? Maybe go on a real date, get to know her better than just sex. Although the sex had been…well, damned good.

She'd taken the decision out of his hands. For all he

knew, she might have known all along where Jake was. She could have lied like Kacee said. Perhaps have set up the kidnapping, maybe even started the fire in the barn. His mind raced with the depth of her supposed duplicity, all of which he couldn't verify without talking to the woman. Damn it! Where was she?

Kacee touched his arm, her face creased into a frown. "You aren't falling for that woman, are you?"

Tate shook his head. "Like you said, I don't know her." But he *wanted* to get to know her.

"You are!" She stepped back. "What are you thinking?"

He pushed a hand through his hair. "I don't know *what* I'm thinking. I swear she's Jake's mother. He looks just like her."

"And he looked just like Beth Kirksey."

"No. Not after seeing Sylvia and Jake together. He has a birthmark just like hers."

"It could be a tattoo."

"I saw it, it's real." He'd run his lips across it, exploring her body a little at a time.

"Great. The mighty Vincent is in lust." Kacee crossed her arms over her chest. "What could you possibly see in her?"

All the thoughts of her fooling him vanished, and the fierce look on her face as she attacked El Corredor from behind flashed in Tate's mind. She'd been like a lioness protecting her pride. Loyal, courageous and tenacious. "She's beautiful."

"Well, don't get carried away, Casanova. In case your memory is slipping along with your common sense, the woman's gone." Kacee's mouth pressed into a thin line. "Did you bring me here for a reason? Because if not, I could be tucked in a bed sleeping."

"We need to call the FBI and report Sylvia missing."

"She hasn't been gone for more than twenty-four hours. Was there a sign of struggle?"

"No."

Kacee shook her head. "The police won't even talk to you."

"Then we have to get to Special Agent Bradley."

"Special Agent Bradley? An FBI agent?"

"Yes."

"What happened to the guy from Austin who was supposed to be investigating the kidnapping?"

"The case has been transferred." He walked to his truck and opened the door. "I need to touch base with her. She might have a lead on the location where the stolen babies are being taken."

Kacee's brows rose. "Really? You think this is more than just a kidnapping of millionaire Tate Vincent's baby for ransom? You bought into all that stuff that Michaels woman told you?"

"Yeah." He glanced at Kacee, his brow furrowing. "You know, on second thought, I'd rather you went back to the ranch. I can speak with the agent on my own. You don't need to be involved with this mess."

"Nice of you to be concerned. I want to be here. I feel somewhat responsible since I found the adoption agency for you." She leaned into his arm and touched his cheek. "I knew how much you wanted a child to carry on the Vincent name."

He captured her hand and held it. "Don't fight me on this, Kacee. Go home." He let go and stepped back, putting distance between them.

She bit down on her lip, her brows drawing together.

He'd seen that look when she'd been ready to launch into an argument.

He held up his hand. "Please, Kacee. Go."

"Is there any chance…you and me…?" She pointed to him and back to herself.

Tate had known for a while that Kacee wanted more than boss-employee relationship. He'd never given her reason to believe he wanted the same. She was a good assistant, one he could hardly do without. "No, Kacee. The most we'll ever be is friends."

Without another word, Kacee spun on her heel and climbed into her car. Before she pulled away, she slid the window down. "If you need me tonight, I'll be at a friend's house."

Something Sylvia had mentioned came to Tate. "Kacee?"

She glanced through the window at him. "Yeah."

"When did your brother get out of jail?"

Her eyes narrowed slightly. "Why do you ask?"

Tate found it interesting that she avoided his question. "Just curious. Is that the friend you're staying with?"

She hesitated. "No, it isn't. I'm not on speaking terms with my brother. Is there a problem?"

His gut tightened, instinct kicking in. He could tell she held back. "No, no. I just wonder why you never told me your brother was out of jail."

"How did you find out?"

"I don't remember. Someone told me in passing," he lied. "Maybe Zach."

Her eyes narrowed even more. "I'll head back to the office tomorrow." She raised the window halfway and then lowered it again. "Tate?"

Tate walked over to her.

She reached out and caught his hand. "You'll regret

this, Tate. Mark my words. That woman isn't the one for you."

Tate nodded. "Maybe not, but I have to find her."

"WHERE IS JACOB?" Sylvia asked as Velvet accelerated onto Loop 410, the inside loop surrounding the center of San Antonio. "Where is my son? And why is it necessary for me to drive around with you?" The longer she remained away from the motel room, the more likely Tate would worry.

"I think someone followed me. I can't stay in one place too long." The prostitute shot a glance to her rearview mirror and another to the side mirror. "Raul doesn't like it when I disappear."

Sylvia clenched her fists to keep from reaching out and shaking the information out of the woman. "What did you find out?"

"I was talking with Candy. She had a baby not long ago and gave it up for adoption." Velvet looked across the console at Sylvia. "She used the same agency as Beth."

"The agency is closed. I've already checked."

Velvet nodded. "I know. Candy talked about El Corredor and how he'd taken her out to the hill country to a private clinic where she could have her baby. She said they had a nursery there with a number of babies, but she didn't see that many mothers. Just nurses or caregivers feeding the babies."

Sylvia's heart leaped. "A private clinic? Where?"

"She wasn't exactly sure. El Corredor had her blindfolded before taking her there and bringing her back."

Another roadblock. Sylvia sat back in her seat, all her excitement fading. "How can I search the entire hill country? How will I ever find it?"

"She didn't know exactly where it was, but she did

see the name of the linen service that delivered to it. She thought maybe that would help."

"Who delivered?"

"Allied Cleaning Services."

"Sounds like a chain."

"No. I checked, they only have an office in Comfort."

Sylvia dared to hope. "Anything else?"

"No. That was all she saw or heard."

"I need a car," Sylvia thought out loud. "I need to get out to Comfort."

"I can drop you at a car rental place."

Sylvia shook her head. "That won't do. I'm broke. I've spent every last penny searching for my son. I have nothing left. Could you drop me back at the motel?"

"No. It's too dangerous. I can let you out at the next gas station and you can call your guy from there."

Velvet pulled off the highway and behind a gas station-convenience store, parking in the shadows.

"Thank you for everything, Velvet. I'm sorry I gave you such a hard time." On impulse, Sylvia leaned across and hugged Velvet.

When she sat back and reached for the door handle, Velvet's hand stopped her. With her other hand, she dug into her cleavage and pulled out a wad of bills. "Here, take this. It'll get you where you need to go."

Sylvia held up her hands. This woman had sold her body for that cash, the hardest-earned paycheck Sylvia could imagine. "I can't take your money."

She took Sylvia's hand and pressed the money into it, folding her fingers around it. "Find your baby. Take him home and be a good mother to him."

"Why are you doing this? I thought you hated me."

Velvet pushed a long strand of black hair behind her

ear and stared off into the night. "Let's just say I've made mistakes. Mistakes I've regretted."

Sylvia stuffed the cash into her pocket and climbed out of the car. She leaned back in. "Thanks, Velvet. I'll pay you back. I promise."

"Just get there in time, will ya?"

Sylvia shut the car door and Velvet sped off. Sylvia pulled her cell phone from her back pocket and pressed the on button. Nothing. She'd keyed Tate's number into her cell phone, but she didn't know it by heart. Without a battery to boot the phone, she didn't have a way to contact him.

She rounded the corner of the convenience store and walked in. She had to pay the guy behind the counter five bucks to convince him to let her use his phone and a phone book.

With time ticking away, Sylvia dialed the number for the motel and asked for their room number. Tate should be back by now. She hadn't had time to leave a note. He'd be mad that she'd left.

The phone rang ten times before Sylvia gave up. Her next call was for a taxi.

When she finally made it back to the motel, an hour had passed. The first thing she noticed was that Tate's truck wasn't there. She used the key card Tate had left with her, letting herself into the room.

Everything was as she'd left it except Tate's gym bag was gone. If the bed hadn't been mussed, she'd swear he'd never been there. With no way to contact him, she didn't have any other choice but to do this on her own. She climbed into the waiting taxi. "Take me to a place where I can rent a car with cash."

Five minutes later, he'd dropped her off at a car rental place near the airport. Without a credit card, she had to bribe the clerk with an additional hundred dollars to get him to sign over a car to her. Knowing how hard Velvet had worked for that cash made Sylvia sick. But she handed it over, grabbed the set of keys and ran for the car.

The sun would be up in a couple of hours. If she wanted to catch the delivery drivers for the cleaning service, she'd have to get there early. If her memory served her well, it would take thirty to forty minutes to get out to Comfort and a few more minutes to find the business.

Afraid to hope, afraid to get excited, Sylvia drove out of the rental car lot, careful not to draw attention to herself. She couldn't afford to get pulled over by a cop. Jacob needed her and she now had a clue as to where he was.

She angled the car for the on ramp to the bypass and pressed her foot to the floor. "I'm coming, Jacob. Hold on, baby."

Chapter Sixteen

"When was the last time you saw her?" Melissa sat across the conference table in the war room of the San Antonio branch of the FBI, a cup of coffee getting cold next to her.

"Over an hour ago." Tate fought to sit still on the cracked-leather conference room chair. "Did you find out anything? Does your inside guy know how to contact El Corredor?"

"He's working on it as we speak. Not that I think he'll get anywhere as late as it is. Plus your activities tonight might have spooked El Corredor." She leaned toward him. "I did enter Velvet's pimp into the system and came up with some names of gang members he hangs with. I also have some pictures our undercover guy made with a concealed camera. Maybe you can identify the men you ran up against."

Melissa opened her laptop. She brought up a photo and turned the screen toward Tate. "Any of these familiar?"

The photo was grainy, but Tate thought two of the men looked familiar. "That's him. That's the guy they call El Corredor. The other is his bodyguard."

"How about in the next picture?"

The next shot had three men gathered around a street

corner in the business district of downtown San Antonio. The light wasn't all that good and Tate had a harder time picking out someone he recognized. He pointed at a man with what looked like a tattoo on his arm. "That's the bodyguard again. And the man with his back to the camera could be El Corredor." He leaned closer. A man with reddish-brown hair stared straight at the camera. "I think I've seen that guy before, but I can't place him."

Melissa zoomed in on the man. "He's one of the guys I needed to talk with you about." She stared across the table at him. "Our agent said this man is Danny LeBlanc. I believe he's related to one of your employees."

Tate's brows furrowed for a moment then cleared. "Would it be Kacee LeBlanc's brother?"

"Yeah. He's in violation of his parole for hanging out with these gang members."

"Do you know where to find him?"

"Based on his parole records, we have the address of the apartment he's supposed to be living in."

"Let's go." Tate stood, pushing back his chair so hard it toppled over backward.

"Wait a minute, Tate. You're not an agent, you're not even a law enforcement official. I can't take you with me."

"Why the hell not?"

"We don't know if he's involved with the whole baby-selling business. Our undercover agent is working it as we speak. Let him do his job."

"I can't stand by and do nothing." Tate moved toward the door of the conference room.

Melissa caught his arm. "Give us time to do our jobs."

He didn't turn to face her, his mind already ahead of him. "Sylvia and Jake may not have time." He shook off her hand and walked out, weaving through the maze of desks and emerging from the building into the gray of predawn.

Kacee's brother was a gang member? Did she know this?

He got out his cell phone and almost hit the speed dial for Kacee when he thought better of it. If Kacee was staying the rest of the night with her brother, she'd be at his apartment. If her brother really was involved with the thugs who'd tried to kill them tonight, he wouldn't want Tate asking questions.

Tate clicked several buttons on his cell phone and brought up the Internet site he used to track the cell phones of the people he employed. He keyed in Kacee's phone number and waited. A map of San Antonio came up with a blinking dot where Kacee's phone was located.

Tate ran for his truck. If he wanted information out of Kacee's brother, he'd better get to him before the FBI agent did. Added to his concern was Kacee, she might be in danger, too.

Meanwhile, the clock was ticking and Sylvia and Jake might be running out of time.

SYLVIA PARKED A block from the cleaners and crept into the building unnoticed. A large delivery van had backed up to a loading dock and two men loaded carts of linens into the back.

Considering how small the town was, the one van probably served all the company's customers. If Sylvia wanted to get into a secret compound, what better way than as a delivery?

When the workers went back inside for another load, Sylvia made her move. She dove into the back of the van and hid behind a rolling cart filled with clean sheets and tablecloths.

Her heart thundered against her ears as she strained to hear movement outside.

"This is the last one," a worker said. A thump jolted the metal floor of the van. The squeak of wheels headed her way had Sylvia ducking low, tugging the corner of a freshly laundered towel over her head. She could just see the tips of black work boots.

Afraid to breathe, afraid to move and alert the worker to her presence, Sylvia waited an eternity for the boots to move. Finally, they left, a metal door slid shut and her world went dark.

The engine revved and the truck lumbered over the rough roads on the way to each of its deliveries. First obstacle overcome, Sylvia managed to fill her lungs and plan for her next move.

After several stops in town, Sylvia began to wonder if there was another truck that had left earlier. There were only two large rollaway carts. If the van was going to make a delivery to the compound, it had to be soon. Hiding between the two carts was no longer an option.

Sylvia stood and moved the sheets, tablecloths and towels around in the cart and carefully climbed over the edge. One by one, she refolded the sheets and stacked them on top of her body and head, completely covering herself.

When the truck jerked to a halt and the engine shut off, Sylvia's heart raced. She prayed she'd gotten on the right van and prayed even harder that Jacob would be in the compound, alive and safe.

The back door slid upward, light spilling through the opening, barely penetrating the cocoon she'd wrapped herself in.

Buried in the cart, she froze, afraid the sheets would shift and expose her.

"Must have extra guests out here. They sent extra linens this time," the worker said as he rolled the cart across the floor of the van.

"No more than usual," another voice said next to cart. "I'll check the invoice once I get inside. Just leave the second one there. I'll come back and get it."

"Will do."

The cart jolted and then rolled easily across a smooth surface.

Now that she was inside the compound, Sylvia hoped that they wouldn't unload the cart immediately, so she could escape undetected.

When the cart quit rolling, Sylvia lay still for several minutes, listening.

The only voices she could detect sounded as if they moved away from her along with the footsteps.

She moved the sheets aside just a bit and peered out of her hiding place. So far so good.

She inched her head up over the top of the bin and looked around at what appeared to be a really big closet filled with bedsheets, towels and tablecloths in neat stacks on shelves against one wall. The other walls were stacked with scrubs, white jackets, surgical garb of varying sizes, toilet paper, paper towels, cleaning supplies and disinfectants.

She heard voices getting louder.

Sylvia climbed out of the cart and dropped behind it. She hurried toward a door that stood open at the far end of the room, ducking behind it as two women dressed in green scrubs entered.

"What's the big push to get all the babies ready to go?"

"I don't know. I think they're transferring them to another location."

"I hope that doesn't mean they're closing this facility. I can't afford to lose this job."

"Me, either. Hate to drive all the way to San Antonio for work."

"Still, all this hush-hush is silly. In this day and age, a woman has the right to give a baby up for adoption without feeling persecuted."

"Yeah, makes you wonder about it all. What with the barbed-wire fences and guards at the gate."

"Shh…here comes Barb. She doesn't like us talking. She jumped down the throat of the new girl when she pulled out her personal cell phone on duty. Thought she'd have a conniption fit."

"That's one of the first things they warned us at orientation—no cell phones inside the gates." The woman grabbed baby blankets from a shelf and handed them to the other. "Here, you better get going."

She took a stack of crib sheets for herself and both women left the room in silence.

A larger, older woman entered. Sylvia guessed this was Barb.

The woman pulled a set of keys away from her waist on a retractable cable and unlocked a sturdy metal cabinet, removed a plastic package of what looked like syringes and a couple of clear glass vials. She left, her rubber-soled shoes squeaking on the yellowing linoleum tiles.

Left alone, Sylvia grabbed green scrubs from a stack on the shelf nearest her and pulled them on over her clothes. She tucked her hair up in a surgical cap and peeked around the door.

The hallway, smelling of disinfectant, stood empty.

Sylvia moved quickly, glancing into open doorways. The rooms appeared like dorm rooms, with built-in dressers, a twin-size bed and plain utilitarian nightstand. Bare bones like a low-cost hospital or a nursing home.

In one room she passed, a young woman was lying on the bed, her belly large and swollen, her face haggard. She was asleep, her arms beside her, lined with needle marks.

Sylvia's heart bled for the girl. Pregnant and addicted. The poor baby would probably be delivered addicted, as well. The world was a harsh enough environment for a baby to live in.

At the end of the hallway, Sylvia glanced around the corner to the right. A couple of women in scrubs wheeled newborns in small carts from a room marked Nursery, walking away from her.

To the left, babies' cries carried through the walls. A door opened and the crying grew louder. One of the women Sylvia had seen in the storage room turned her way.

Sylvia ducked back down the hallway she'd come from and into an empty room.

As she waited for the woman's footsteps to pass by, she listened to the noise through the wall.

These babies didn't sound like newborns. They had heartier lungs, like those of older children.

Hope leaped in her chest. Somehow, she had to get inside that room. Jacob could be there.

When the footsteps faded, Sylvia hurried out into the hall and turned the corner toward the room where the babies were crying.

"Hey!" a woman yelled. "Who locked the exit door?" A door at the end of the hallway behind her rattled. "Anyone know who locked this door?"

Women emerged from doorways lining the corridor, some in scrubs, some in nightgowns, sporting enormous pregnant bellies.

Another staff member joined the woman at the locked doorway and attempted to push the double doors open, but they remained jammed shut.

"Let me try the one at the other end of the hall," another staff member called out and turned toward where Sylvia stood.

She marched toward the other end of the passage. When she passed Sylvia, she frowned. "Are you new around here?"

Sylvia nodded, remembering that she wore scrubs like the majority of the staff.

The woman didn't stop, but said over her shoulder, "Give me a hand then."

Sylvia fell into step behind her, passing the room where the babies still cried.

When she reached the double doors at the end of the corridor, the staff member pushed on the lever. It depressed as it should, but the door didn't open.

"It's jammed. Help me push on it."

Sylvia leaned against the door at the same time as the other woman. The door refused to budge.

"That's odd. This is an emergency exit, locked from the inside. It shouldn't be locked from the outside."

Standing next to the woman, Sylvia prayed she didn't question her more on her employment. All she wanted was to get into the room with the crying babies and find Jacob.

"Smoke! I smell smoke!" The very pregnant woman with the track marks on her arms, ran out into the main hall, screaming.

Fire alarms went off and soon the halls were filled with young women, nurses and clinic staff.

"We can't open any of the doors. They're all blocked!" a young nurse cried out.

"Call the fire department!" Barb, the head nurse, yelled.

A woman leaned over a desk and picked up the telephone. "No signal."

"Someone have a cell phone?"

"No, we aren't allowed to have cell phones here."

Gray tendrils of smoke seeped through the walls, rising in the air.

Sylvia's heart raced, her lungs still scratchy from her last bout of arson. No longer caring whether or not she was found out, she pushed through the doorway into the room with the crying babies, at the same time as two women ran out.

Playpens lined the walls, each with a small child, either standing or sitting inside. All were crying. There had to be at least ten babies in the room.

None of them had light blond hair and blue eyes. Sylvia checked every playpen thoroughly, searching beneath blankets for the one child she'd never given up on. When she reached the last playpen, it was empty. A bottle lay on the mat inside, empty. Where was the child?

A stuffed toy lay on the floor. Sylvia leaned over the playpen. A golden-haired child sat there, shaking a ragged plush toy. "Jacob?" He looked up at her and shook the toy again, giggling.

"Jacob!" She jerked the playpen from the wall and grabbed the baby into her arms. "Oh, God, Jacob." Tears ran down her face.

He patted her cheeks with the toy, his brows drawing together. "Da, da, da."

"Oh, baby, yes. We'll get out of here and you can see your daddy." Sylvia coughed, suddenly aware of the screams from the hallway and the increase of smoke in the baby room. If she could open a window, maybe the smoke would clear. Hopefully they had the fire under control by now.

Based on the amount of noise in the hallway, she didn't think that was a possibility.

Sylvia's gaze darted around the room, noticing for the first time a lack of windows. For that matter, none of the dorm rooms she'd passed had windows.

A woman burst through the doorway. "We have to get these babies out of here. The entire building is on fire!"

Sylvia grabbed another child from a playpen, balancing one on each hip, and she raced out into the hall crowded with staff and pregnant women.

The nurses and patients huddled close to the floors where the smoke wasn't so bad, sobbing. "We can't get out. We're trapped," one patient cried.

Carrying the babies on her hips, Sylvia hurried down the hallway, checking room after room for a window. There weren't any. Flames ate their way in from the outside, burning through the siding and framework. Someone had built the place like a fortress.

Or a tomb.

TATE FOUND KACEE'S CAR parked in the parking lot of a run-down apartment building. He couldn't possibly knock on every door to find the right one. It would give Danny time to figure it out and run.

Climbing down from his truck, Tate found a position

behind a bush close to the middle of the building. Staircases on either side led to the parking lot. If Danny lived on the bottom floor, he'd just have to run faster than him.

In position and ready, he dialed Kacee's number.

"Tate? Why are you still up? Did you find the Michaels woman?"

"Where are you right now?"

"Why?" she asked.

"Just want to make sure you got to your friend's apartment safely."

"I am."

"This friend male or female?"

Kacee laughed. "So now you're interested?"

"Not for the reasons you'd think."

A long pause ensued, then Kacee sighed. "What are you talking about, Tate?"

"Did I tell you that I had all the business phones placed on a GPS scanning system in case we lost one?"

A crackling sound came to Tate through the receiver, and muffled voices he couldn't understand. Kacee had her hand over the speaker.

"Where are you, Tate?"

"Close by. Mind if I come meet your friend?"

"It's really late. Besides, she stepped out a minute ago."

"I thought you said she was sick?"

A door opened and a man slipped out of a second-floor apartment and raced for the staircase.

"Okay, then, I'll see you back at the office." He clicked the off button and slipped the phone in his pocket.

Keeping low and behind the vehicles in the parking lot, Tate raced across the pavement, arriving at the base of the stairs as the man reached the bottom.

Tate hit him like a linebacker, catching him in the gut and knocking him flat on his back.

The man struggled, his arms and legs flailing out to the sides, but Tate had him pinned.

"Danny LeBlanc, right?"

The man stilled. "You got the wrong guy."

Tate leaned back, and a beam from a nearby streetlight crossed over the man's face. The face he hadn't been able to place until now. Kacee had a photo of a younger version of this guy in her wallet. She'd dropped it one day when she'd been rifling through her purse for a pen.

"Where are they?"

"Where are who?"

"Where does El Corredor keep the babies?"

"I don't know what you're talking about."

Tate pulled his gun out of the back of his jeans and held it to the man's temple. "I don't feel like arguing."

Danny snorted. "You won't shoot."

"Try me." Tate's anger and fear consumed him. He could barely see the man in front of him for the red shadowing his vision. "All you are is one more obstacle in the way of getting my son back."

"Stop!" Kacee rushed down the steps, hair flying, her blouse untucked and makeup smeared. "Don't hurt him."

"Stay where you are or I'll shoot him," Tate warned.

"Go ahead." Danny laughed. "Shoot me."

"No!" Kacee ran down a couple more steps, tripped and plowed into Tate, knocking him off his feet and flat on his back. His wrist hit the ground, and the Sig Sauer flew from his fingertips and slid beneath a car.

"Danny isn't to blame, don't hurt him." Kacee clutched at Danny's shirt, pulling him against her chest. "I made him find Jake to begin with, and then I made him take Jake away."

"Shut up, Kacee." Danny rolled to the side, placing Kacee between him and Tate.

"It's all my fault," she blubbered, her voice catching on her sobs. "I started the fire so that Danny would have a chance to steal Jake."

"Why?" Tate inched his way back toward the car where his gun lay.

"Don't you see? I love you," she cried, her eyes filled with tears.

"I told you to shut up." Danny's arm circled Kacee's neck and he squeezed hard, cutting off her air.

Tate dove under the car, grabbed the gun and rolled to his feet, aiming at the man's head. "Let her go, Danny."

"No, I can't." He squeezed harder.

Kacee kicked and flailed, her eyes wide, pleading, her face turning a sickly shade of blue.

"Put the gun down or I'll kill her." Danny tightened his hold on her neck.

If he hesitated any longer, Kacee would die. Tate laid the gun down on the pavement.

"Kick it to the side," Danny demanded.

Tate kicked the weapon out of reach.

"You rich guys want it all and have the money to pay for it. You can even buy children no one else wants." He stood, bringing Kacee up with him, her feet dangling off the ground.

"Put Kacee down, Danny. She's not the one you want to hurt."

"Selling kids to the rich people beats hell out of growing up abandoned, living out of Dumpsters and fighting for everything you have."

Kacee's struggles weakened, her body going limp.

Tate threw himself at the pair, knocking them to the ground.

Danny's head cracked against the stairs and he lay motionless. Kacee rolled to the side, at first still, then her chest heaved and she sucked in a deep breath. She coughed and drew in more air. When the color returned to her face, she crawled over to her brother. "Danny? Oh, Danny." She laid her cheek against his chest. "You're going to be okay, I promise. I'll get us out of this mess."

Blood pooled on the concrete sidewalk beneath Danny's head. Tate felt his neck for a pulse. It was weak.

Kacee sobbed against her brother's chest. "You killed him." She pushed up and threw herself at Tate, scratching and clawing. "You killed him!" she repeated.

"He was killing you, Kacee. If I hadn't stopped him, you'd be dead. Besides, this idiot's not dead."

"He didn't mean it. He's all the family I have. He didn't mean it."

"Kacee, he's alive, will you listen to me?" Tate pulled her into his arms and held her until the sobs subsided. Then he pushed her to arm's length and brushed the hair out of her face. "I'll get him some help, but you have to tell me where they are. Where are the babies El Corredor steals?"

"I don't know." She shook her head, staring down at the brother she so obviously loved.

"You have to know. You're the only one left who can tell me. Please, Kacee, tell me." He shook her gently, but firmly. "Tell me now."

"Out near Comfort." She tried to pull away. "Leave me alone. You never wanted me. No one ever wanted us." Kacee lay down beside Danny's body, moaning.

Tate lifted her up enough to face him. "Where in Comfort?"

She stared up at him, her eyes swimming. "That's all I know."

Tate stood and yanked his cell phone from his pocket. He punched the speed dial number for Agent Bradley.

"Bradley speaking."

"Comfort. They keep the babies somewhere out near Comfort."

"I was just about to call you. I got word from my undercover agent. He said that El Corredor left an hour ago, saying he had to take care of evidence. He followed him to a compound out near Comfort, but it's fenced and under armed guard. I'm on my way to the airport. Meet me there and you can ride with me in the chopper."

"I'll be there in five." He clicked the off button. "I'm calling the paramedics. Stay with him until they get here."

"I'm not going anywhere. He didn't leave me when our mother did." She held Danny's hand in hers. "I won't leave him. He's my brother."

Tate climbed into his truck, pressing 9-1-1 as he drove out of the parking lot.

When he reached the airport, he called Melissa's cell phone and stayed on with her until he found the helicopter pad.

Within minutes, the bird took off, headed toward the hill country northwest of San Antonio.

Melissa handed him a headset, settling hers over her ears.

As they passed over the small German town of Boerne, Tate leaned forward. A plume of smoke rose from one of the rolling hills ahead.

"We have a fire ahead," the pilot informed them.

"Just got a text from our man on the ground." Melissa leaned over the pilot's shoulder, scanning the horizon. "Looks like the compound is on fire. We have backup on the way, but they might not get there in time. Hurry!"

The helicopter swooped in over the barbed-wire fences, the heat from the flames buffeting the blades, making it difficult to land.

Guard towers stood empty and deserted. Surrounded by a wall of smoke and flame, they were hardly visible.

As soon as Tate dropped down out of the helicopter, he smelled the acrid scent of gasoline. Someone had set the fire. The question foremost in his mind made his stomach roil. Were there people still inside?

Flames crackled and roared, drowning out almost every other noise. But as soon as the helicopter lifted off and away from the burning building, screams could be heard.

His heart stopped for two whole beats before it slammed against his chest, blasting blood and adrenalin through his veins.

Two vehicles pulled out from behind the building. A black Hummer and a silver Suburban.

Tate, Melissa and two other agents stood in the path between the vehicles and the gate leading out of the compound. All four of them had weapons drawn.

"Wait until they're within range!" Melissa called out.

As the vehicles drew near, a man leaned out of the Hummer wielding a submachine gun.

Tate and the agents dropped to the ground and opened fire.

The front windshield shattered and the driver swerved to the right. The second vehicle sped up.

Tate unloaded his clip, aiming for the driver of the Suburban. The agents peppered the vehicle, some aiming for the tires. The Suburban kept coming. At the last minute, the driver's head jerked back, a bullet through the windshield finally stopping him. The vehicle swerved sharply and flipped, tumbling straight for Tate.

Tate dove to the side and rolled out of the way, the whoosh of air, shattering glass and the thunder of a ton of metal pounded the ground where he'd been. The Suburban crashed against the limestone fence and burst into flame.

Screams from inside the building grew louder.

"Leave them!" Melissa shouted, running for the building, dropping her empty clip and reloading as she ran.

Tate tossed his empty pistol to the ground and raced to catch up. Hands pounded the metal emergency exit from the inside, their voices desperate and frightened. A chain wrapped around the handles barred anyone from entering or leaving.

"Stand back!" Mel placed her Glock against the lock, turned her face away and pulled the trigger. The hasp exploded and Tate jerked the chains free.

When he opened the door, smoke billowed out. Women rushed past him, some pregnant, others carrying babies. They dove for the fresh clean air, coughing and gasping. Melissa and her agents helped those who couldn't make it on their own and rushed back in to help more.

Tate ran past one woman after another. No sign of Sylvia or Jake. This was not happening. He couldn't lose Jake, the boy he loved as his own. He wanted a chance to get to know Sylvia, the courageous woman who'd come to mean more than he'd ever thought possible in such a short amount of time.

Smoke choked his throat and lungs, but he pressed

on, pulling his shirt up over his mouth. His eyes burned as he worked his way into the clinic.

"Sylvia!" he yelled into the roiling smoke. "Sylvia!"

"Here! We're in here!"

Tate rounded a corner, running crouched over to stay below the rising smoke.

"In here!" Sylvia cried again.

Tate burst through a door, tripped over a pile of baby blankets and ground to a halt.

Sylvia had a playpen full of babies a few feet from the door. "I couldn't leave them."

In her arms, Jake clung to her, his face streaked with tears. When he saw Tate, he held out his arms.

"Oh, Jake. Baby, come to Daddy." Tate gathered the child into his arms and hugged him tight, a lump rising in his throat. He pulled Sylvia against him with his other arm and kissed her forehead, unable to speak.

She clung to his shirt, tears wetting the fabric, never more happy to see someone. "Thank God you found us." She smiled up at him, blinking back the tears, smoke stinging her eyes, burning her lungs.

"You scared the crud out of me." He kissed her forehead and touched his lips to hers.

She kissed him back, liking the feel of him against her, until the smoke coughed it out of her. "I blocked the door to keep the smoke from coming in, but we have to get out now or we won't make it." Sylvia pushed away from him, her eyes wide as she spied the rising flames licking at the hallway walls.

Tate glanced at the playpen full of babies all around Jake's age. "We can't carry all the babies out one at a time."

"Then you get one side of the playpen and I'll get the other. We can drag it out with all of them in it."

Tate set Jake in the pen. The little guy screamed, coughed and sat down, sobbing.

Sylvia's heart broke for him, but she couldn't take time to get him out and make it back for the rest. And she'd be damned if she left even one of them. Flames leaped in the hallway. Flames they'd have to run through in order to get the babies out. She squared her shoulders, pulled her shirt up over her mouth and shouted above the roar of the encroaching fire. "I've wet the blankets. Toss them over the babies." Sylvia lifted the wet blankets she'd used to seal the cracks around the door frame and threw them over the crying babies. Tate scrambled to get the rest thrown over the kids.

Each adult grabbed the sides of the playpen and they half lifted, half carried the pen through the double-wide doorway and out into the hallway.

Flames climbed the walls, eating at the wallpaper, making it curl up. Smoke as black as night choked the air.

"Get down!" Tate yelled and coughed, dropping to his knees.

Sylvia dropped low, but she couldn't get enough leverage on her knees. Eight babies and the playpen were heavy and tough going in the smoky hallway.

Her lungs burned, every inch a challenge, but she had to make it, had to get the babies out of this nightmare.

With renewed effort, she got behind the playpen, braced her feet on the base and shoved as hard as she could. With Tate pulling at the front and her pushing from behind, they made it to the end of the hallway.

Two men and a woman materialized through the smoke.

Tate yelled to them, "Grab the playpen and get it out of here."

The four of them lifted the playpen and ran out of the building.

With the babies safely out of the building, Sylvia was exhausted. She leaned against the wall, her feet splayed out in front of her. Unable to lift a finger, the effort of pushing the playpen and inhaling all that smoke had sapped every last ounce of energy. She was cooked.

She closed her eyes and lay on the tile, the heat of the fire behind her growing more intense. But she couldn't move. None of her muscles cooperated. Jacob was okay, that's all that mattered.

Blackness surrounded her, filling her lungs, dragging her away into a dark abyss. Then she was floating through the smoke, the heat dissipating, the wall she'd leaned against not quite as hard, but steely strong.

Breathing became easier and she inhaled a lung full of clean fresh air, which sent her into a coughing fit she thought would never end.

Someone pressed a mask over her face. "Breathe, Sylvia, breathe."

She stopped struggling, inhaled deeply and opened her eyes.

Tate stood over her, the sunlight bright and hopeful behind him. He held an oxygen mask over her face. She pushed it aside. "Jake?"

"He's okay." Melissa Bradley appeared beside Tate with Jake in her arms. "He wants his daddy." She handed him to Tate.

Sirens blared as fire engines and emergency vehicles rolled into the compound. Emergency personnel dropped out of them, running toward the people lying on the grass.

"Did everyone get out?" Sylvia asked, amazed at how hoarse she sounded.

"You were the last one." Tate sat on the grass beside her, Jake in his arms. "Everyone's out, and all the children are accounted for."

Jake leaned over, determined to sit in the grass with the adults.

Tate set him down and the little boy immediately began plucking at blades of grass, giggling. His face dirty with soot, his nose running and generally a mess, he was the most beautiful creature on earth to Sylvia. Her heart filled so full she thought it might burst.

Sylvia smiled, her gaze still on her son. "Thank you for saving us." She tried to push into a sitting position, but Tate held her back.

"Stay here until the medics have a chance to check you out."

"But I'm fine except for a little smoke inhalation."

"A little?" Tate cupped her chin, his brown-black eyes bloodshot from all the smoke. "Please."

"Okay." She lay against the grass, staring up at Tate. "Did you find out who set the fire?"

"El Corredor and some of his pals." Tate nodded toward the fence where a vehicle lay on its side. Another stood in the middle of the compound, windows shattered. The local sheriff's department and what looked like FBI agents removed bodies from inside both of them, laying them out on the ground. "They won't be trafficking babies anymore."

Sylvia closed her eyes. "You've been busy."

"You scared a few years off my life." He lifted her hand and pressed it to his cheek. "When I saw the fire…"

"*I* scared *you?*" She laughed, another fit of coughing racked her lungs. "Well, we all made it through and the babies are safe. What now?"

Jake used Tate's sleeve and pulled himself into a standing position, giggling and slapping at Tate's arm. "Da, da, da."

Tate smiled down at him. "That's right, buddy. You don't look the worse for your experience. Ready to go home, little man?" As if he just remembered, Tate's gaze shot to Sylvia. "That's if you two would stay with me until we can figure this whole thing out."

"Do you still believe I'm not Jacob's mother?"

Tate lips twisted. "Any woman who'd go through what you did would have to be the baby's mother." Tate lifted Jake in his arms and stared into the baby's blue eyes. "Besides, he looks like you."

"I can't take your charity."

"Then let me hire you."

"For what?"

"As my executive assistant."

"But you already have one."

Tate's mouth pressed into a straight line. "Not anymore." He explained Kacee and Danny's role in Jake's abduction.

"I almost feel sorry for her. To love the man you work for and him not return the feeling..." Sylvia looked away. "I don't know about this position."

"Do you have a job?"

"No."

"I'm offering you work. I pay well, and one of the perks is a place to live for both you and Jake."

Jake climbed into Tate's lap and lay down, working at the button on the man's shirt as his eyes drifted shut.

Her son loved this man he'd grown to know as his father. How could she take him away?

"Mind if I take Jake for a minute?" Melissa reappeared and took Jake from Tate's lap. "The EMTs want to give him a once-over."

The silence she left behind was as thick as the smoke inside the building.

Sylvia valued her independence and wanted to make her life work on her own. Relying on a man had only gotten her into trouble.

If she went to work for Tate, would she be falling into the same trap? "I can't work for you. I'd feel like a charity case. Besides, I want to pursue my freelance writing. It's what I do best."

"Then let me help until you get on your feet."

Sylvia chewed her lip. She needed to build up her portfolio and contacts again. She'd be starting from nothing. No photos, no database of articles she'd written, not even a home to bring Jacob to. What kind of life could she provide for her son?

Then again, to work with Tate and not be anything more than an employee? After what they'd been through, all that they'd shared in the past two days...to be so close and not touch him would just about kill her. "I've never been an executive assistant," she said, afraid to voice all of her other reservations when all she'd done since she'd met Tate was keep him at emotional arm's length.

Until the smoke and fire threatened to kill her, she hadn't realized that she wanted more than a no-commitment relationship. She wanted more from Tate Vincent than a romp in the sack, although that had been good. Real good.

She could actually picture herself with him for the long haul. The grow-old and rock-on-the-porch togetherness she'd never felt with her first husband. "I need to think about this."

"Come live with me until you get on your feet." He

took her hand and pulled her into his arms. "Do it for Jake. Do it for me. I want to get to know you, Sylvia Michaels."

She smiled, her lips trembling. "Only because of Jacob."

He frowned. "No, not just because of Jake."

"But you're Tate Vincent, multimillionaire and most eligible bachelor in the state of Texas. What do I have to offer in a relationship?"

"Don't you see?" He kissed her forehead. "When it comes down to it, I'm only a man." A work-roughened hand smoothed the hair out of her face and tucked it behind her ear. "And you're one of the bravest women I know."

"How will I know you want me around for me and not just to keep Jacob?" she whispered.

"Do you have any idea how beautiful you are?" He kissed the tip of her nose.

Sylvia laughed, raising a hand to her sooty hair. "I'm a mess."

"The most beautiful mess I've ever seen." His mouth descended and claimed hers, his tongue pushing past her lips to find hers, stroking her, thrusting deep.

Sylvia had never experienced a kiss so tender and yet so filled with passion. She could die in his arms right there and know that he was the best thing to ever happen to her.

When he ended the kiss, he leaned his forehead against hers. "Sylvia, I'm not perfect. I've been in one bad marriage, but I haven't given up on it altogether."

"I thought I had," she said and pressed a finger to his lips, tracing the sensuous line. "But you make me feel... hopeful."

"I want the time to get to know you. I want to date

you and woo you like a man should with the woman he's falling in love with."

Her heart fluttered. She forgot to breathe. Tate had mentioned the *L* word. Warmth spread through her body in a rush. She tried to tell herself to be calm, review the facts. Make an informed decision from the mind, not the heart.

If she left with Jacob now, she'd never see Tate again. Never know the feel of his arms holding her. Never know if they had a chance to make a life together work. Her rational thoughts told her to grab for happiness. Her heart echoed the sentiment with a thundering pulse.

"Sylvia, will you give me a chance to get to know you? Do you think you can live with me?"

Sylvia's lips trembled as she reached up to cup his chin. "I do." As soon as the two words popped out of her mouth, she gasped, her face burning. "I mean, I accept your proposal…er, offer." She took a deep breath to gather her jumbled thoughts. "But only until I can afford to support myself. And I promise to pay you back for everything."

"Whatever you want."

"I want to come into a relationship with you as an equal." She laughed. "Well, maybe not in millions of dollars, but knowing that I come into the relationship because I want to, not because I have no other choice." She touched the side of his face. "Don't you see?"

"Actually," he said, touching his lips to hers, "I do see. And it makes me want you even more. I think I'm in love and I want the chance to prove it to you."

"And I want the chance to show you that I can love you with or without your riches."

He kissed her, holding her close.

Finally she pushed him away from her. "As far as a

date? How does a Friday-night movie sound? I'll let you choose."

Tate's eyes lit up and his face split into a grin as big as the state of Texas. He hugged her to him and laughed out loud. "Sounds about as close to heaven as we can get."

* * * * *

Silhouette *Desire*

COMING NEXT MONTH

Available September 14, 2010

LARGER-PRINT BOOKS!

GET 2 FREE LARGER-PRINT NOVELS

PLUS 2 FREE GIFTS!

HARLEQUIN®

INTRIGUE®

Breathtaking Romantic Suspense

YES! Please send me 2 FREE LARGER-PRINT Harlequin Intrigue® novels and my 2 FREE gifts (gifts are worth about $10). After receiving them, if I don't wish to receive any more books, I can return the shipping statement marked "cancel." If I don't cancel, I will receive 6 brand-new novels every month and be billed just $4.99 per book in the U.S. or $5.74 per book in Canada. That's a saving of at least 13% off the cover price! It's quite a bargain! Shipping and handling is just 50¢ per book.* I understand that accepting the 2 free books and gifts places me under no obligation to buy anything. I can always return a shipment and cancel at any time. Even if I never buy another book from Harlequin, the two free books and gifts are mine to keep forever.

199/399 HDN E5MS

Name _____ (PLEASE PRINT)

Address _____ Apt. #

City _____ State/Prov. _____ Zip/Postal Code

Signature (if under 18, a parent or guardian must sign)

Mail to the **Harlequin Reader Service:**
IN U.S.A.: P.O. Box 1867, Buffalo, NY 14240-1867
IN CANADA: P.O. Box 609, Fort Erie, Ontario L2A 5X3

Not valid for current subscribers to Harlequin Intrigue Larger-Print books.

Are you a subscriber to Harlequin Intrigue books and want to receive the larger-print edition? Call 1-800-873-8635 today!

* Terms and prices subject to change without notice. Prices do not include applicable taxes. N.Y. residents add applicable sales tax. Canadian residents will be charged applicable provincial taxes and GST. Offer not valid in Quebec. This offer is limited to one order per household. All orders subject to approval. Credit or debit balances in a customer's account(s) may be offset by any other outstanding balance owed by or to the customer. Please allow 4 to 6 weeks for delivery. Offer available while quantities last.

Your Privacy: Harlequin Books is committed to protecting your privacy. Our Privacy Policy is available online at www.eHarlequin.com or upon request from the Reader Service. From time to time we make our lists of customers available to reputable third parties who may have a product or service of interest to you. ☐ If you would prefer we not share your name and address, please check here.

Help us get it right—We strive for accurate, respectful and relevant communications. To clarify or modify your communication preferences, visit us at www.ReaderService.com/consumerchoice.

HILP10R

Enjoy a sneak peek at fan favorite Molly O'Keefe's
Harlequin Superromance miniseries,
THE NOTORIOUS O'NEILLS, *with*
TYLER O'NEILL'S REDEMPTION,
available September 2010
only from Harlequin Superromance.

Police chief Juliette Tremblant recognized the shape of the man strolling down the street—in as calm and leisurely fashion as if it were the middle of the day rather than midnight. She slowed her car, convinced her eyes were playing tricks on her. It had been a long time since Tyler O'Neill had been seen in this town.

As she pulled to a stop at the curb, he turned toward her, and her heart about stopped.

"What the hell are you doing here, Tyler?"

"Well, if it isn't Juliette Tremblant." He made his way over to her, then leaned down so he could look her in the eye. He was close enough to touch.

Juliette was not, repeat, *not* going to touch Tyler O'Neill. Not with her fingers. Not with a ten-foot pole. There would be no touching. Which was too bad, since it was the only way she was ever going to convince herself the man standing in front of her—as rumpled and heart-stoppingly handsome now as he'd been at sixteen—was real.

And not a figment of all her furious revenge dreams.

"What are you doing back in Bonne Terre?" she asked.

"The manor is sitting empty," Tyler said and shrugged as though his arriving out of the blue after ten years was casual. "Seems like someone should be watching over the family home."

"You?" She laughed at the very notion of him being here for any unselfish reason. "Please."

He stared at her for a second, then smiled. Her heart fluttered against her chest—a small mechanical bird powered by that smile.

"You're right." But that cryptic comment was all he offered.

Juliette bit her lip against the other questions.

Why did you go?

Why didn't you write? Call?

What did I do?

But what would be the point? Ten years of silence were all the answer she really needed.

She had sworn off feeling anything for this man long ago. Yet one look at him and all the old hurt and rage resurfaced as though they'd been waiting for the chance. That made her mad.

She put the car in gear, determined not to waste another minute thinking about Tyler O'Neill. "Have a good night, Tyler," she said, liking all the cool "go screw yourself" she managed to fit into those words.

It seems Juliette has an old score to settle with Tyler.
Pick up TYLER O'NEILL'S REDEMPTION
to see how he makes it up to her.
Available September 2010,
only from Harlequin Superromance.

Silhouette

Desire

New York Times and **USA TODAY**
bestselling author

BRENDA JACKSON

brings you

WHAT A WESTMORELAND WANTS,

another seductive Westmoreland tale.

Part of the Man of the Month series

Callum is hopeful that once he gets
Gemma Westmoreland on his native turf
he will wine and dine her with a seduction plan
he has been working on for years—one that
guarantees to make her his.

Available September wherever books are sold.

**Look for a new Man of the Month
by other top selling authors each month.**

Always Powerful, Passionate and Provocative.